BEFORE HIM

CUBS FOR RENT #4

CHARITY PARKERSON

Punk
&
Sissy

--Warning: This book is intended for readers over the age of 18.

INTRODUCTION

KEVIN HAD GIVEN UP ON LIFE BEFORE JERICHO. NOW HE'LL STOP AT NOTHING TO RECLAIM HIMSELF.

For years, Kevin lived in a full-time Dom/sub relationship with his ex. It was a position his ex used to keep Kevin weak and malleable. Now he's free from all that, but he's not whole anymore. He let those years break something inside him that Kevin doesn't know how to fix. Meeting Jericho changes everything.

Before Kevin, Jericho didn't date men. He didn't date anyone. Jericho spent his life focused on his son. Now his son is grown and married, leaving Jericho to find himself again. He thinks working for Cubs for Rent will force him back into the world of single adults. Instead, Jericho can't stop gravitating toward Kevin. He's slightly terrified of what that could mean.

Kevin and Jericho are both starting from a place of having nothing to offer. For different reasons, they're both a bad bet. But sometimes a gamble pays out big winnings. If only one would take the first chance.

PROLOGUE

Author Note

EVEN THOUGH I gave you a small peek into Kevin's life at the end of book three, I'm backing up a little so you can see what happened when Jericho followed Kevin to his car after Mister's blow up. I don't want you to miss any of the good parts. Enjoy!

ONE

THE NIGHT TOBY and Loyal eloped...

A hint of sadness wormed its way into Kevin's heart as he realized this would truly be his last date with Toby. While it was true he paid Toby to spend time with him, the guy still felt like a friend. It was equally hard to swallow that this would be his last date period. Kevin was closing the door on this part of his life. Maybe having no personal life whatsoever would hurt, but Kevin already lived in constant pain. At least, without dating, he would know that pain was self-inflicted. It was too hard to keep slamming himself against the rocks for Mister's sake. Gah. He hated when Haven resurfaced as Mister in his mind. They had been together for several years. At first, it had been beautiful. Kevin had gladly called Haven his Mister. Their relationship had been full-time Dom/Sub. At the time, Kevin had wanted that. He had felt secure in that dynamic. Haven kept him safe. Until the day came that Haven's love started to hurt. His punishment was no longer about discipline. It was control so Kevin would feel too small to leave, even as Haven gave his heart to someone else. His gut churned at the memories. Kevin still felt small. It was well past the time he should accept that the damage was permanent. Being with someone new meant passing that hurt on to a new victim. So he would stop.

Meeting Toby's gorgeous man made his decision more real. He was doing the right thing, Kevin reminded himself as they shook hands.

"I'm Loyal."

Kevin's smile hitched up. It felt so goddamn fake. "Love the name."

"That's a compliment for me," a guy behind Loyal called out, dragging Kevin's attention his way. Kevin had to take a breath. He was so tall and solid. Beautiful. "I'm his dad," the guy explained. His blush turned Kevin's smile real. Kevin understood that one reaction more than anyone there. Everyone else looked confident. Kevin always felt awkward and unsure. Yet this huge and gorgeous man was obviously embarrassed. Kevin couldn't look away as the man fought valiantly to wave away any attention coming his way. "Ignore me. I've been drinking."

Kevin wanted to save him. "There's no way you're old enough to be his father. I call bullshit."

The guy's blush deepened. "I'm a firefighter. I have to stay in shape. Seriously, you can stop me anytime and save me from myself." It was fucking odd. In the span of twenty seconds, Kevin connected more with this guy's awkwardness than he had with anyone in ages. "I'm Jericho, by the way. If you haven't eaten, we're grilling out, if you'd like to join us."

Kevin had already eaten, but he was tempted to stay. He fully recognized he had just decided to bury his heart. Maybe this wasn't about his heart, per se. Possibly, Jericho could be a friend. In truth, Kevin had no clue what it was about the man that intrigued him. There was just some spark of something in Kevin's gut. He couldn't look away from the guy. Blond and beautiful. Kevin didn't know how else to describe him.

The back door opened, pulling Kevin's gaze toward the house before he could respond to Jericho's invitation. Haven stepped out. Everything inside Kevin went cold. Logically, Kevin realized he had known Haven worked for Cubs for Rent. In his heart, he had believed the trio of brothers who ran the company were too good to hang out with Haven outside of offering his services. The Kodiak brothers were nice people. Haven was not. Everything looked ugly in that moment. Kevin lost the ability to hear. His heart beat too loud. He was back on his knees, begging for Haven to see him as human. To treat him better than he would a homeless person on the street. Kevin was back to being less than nothing to the person he loved most in the world. He couldn't breathe. Haven looked outraged. His lips moved and angry words fell, but Kevin couldn't hear a thing over the ugly litany in his head. Goddamn, seeing Haven hurt every fucking time as badly as the last. He hated him.

Kevin turned away. He didn't bother saying goodbye. There was no one there who understood the simmering rage in his gut. There were no words strong enough to describe the way he felt. Kevin didn't owe anyone anything, especially at the cost of his sanity.

"Kevin. Hold up. Stay and talk to me. You don't need to drive like this."

Some of the words chasing him down the driveway finally penetrated Kevin's inner panic. He glanced over his shoulder. To his surprise, it was Jericho on his heels. The shock slowed him. The concern etching Jericho's features froze Kevin's feet to the ground. He looked kind. Fuck, Kevin needed some kindness in his life.

"I'm sorry."

A deep line appeared between Jericho's brows. "Why are you apologizing? You're not the one who just showed his ass back there." Kevin didn't know what he was talking about. He didn't want to admit that he hadn't heard a word exchanged after seeing Haven's face. Jericho kept talking, saving him. "I don't really know Mister. We only met the other day, but he just gave me a very low opinion of him. Are you okay?"

"His name is Haven." Even Kevin heard the disconnect in his voice. He hoped he didn't faint. That was always humiliating.

Jericho moved closer. "I didn't know. He introduced himself to me as Mister."

Life darkened a bit around the edges. Kevin leaned against the driver's side door of his car. The prospects of staying conscious were looking grim. "That's a power trip for him. His subs call him Mister. He likes it. That's why I can't do it." Kevin bent at the waist and sucked air. He hated looking weak. Haven always made him look like a pussy.

A cool hand touched the back of his neck. Air filled Kevin's lungs. "It's okay." Goddamn. Jericho sounded nice. He missed people being nice for no reason at all. "Your heart is beating too fast. Let's find a place for you to sit down."

Kevin squeezed his eyes shut and waved off Jericho's suggestion. "It's okay. Just give me a second." He took a breath, mentally willing his heart to slow. "I have a problem with my heart. This will pass. I just need a minute." Fucking Haven. This was his fault in more ways than one. Kevin had been in great health when they had started dating. All the years of immense stress had literally damaged Kevin's heart. Now, too much stress mimicked a heart attack for him. He was fine. Kevin just needed to calm down. He would not let Haven kill him.

Jericho got down on his haunches so he could meet Kevin's stare. Kevin found himself staring into the most amazing eyes. While holding Kevin's stare, Jericho stood, coaxing Kevin into straightening along with him. Kevin didn't think he had ever been so captivated by someone that his body followed their lead without a single word exchanged. The awkward person Kevin met earlier was gone. This version of

Jericho was confident and in charge. He took care of people. This was obviously his turf. He held Kevin's wrist. It took Kevin a second to realize Jericho was keeping an eye on Kevin's pulse.

"Don't worry," Jericho said, mesmerizing him with his soothing voice. "I won't let anything happen to you." Kevin felt safe. Listening to Jericho speak was like getting a massage. Kevin felt his muscles relax. "I've known the Kodiak boys for all their adult lives. They brought you to their home. Toby introduced you to my son who he would protect with his life. Those boys obviously think you're worth inviting into their lives. You didn't deserve what happened here tonight. Please don't leave here thinking you're not wanted." The way Jericho held Kevin's stare had Kevin incapable of blinking. Jericho's voice lowered a little more, turning downright addictive. "In fact, I'd like for you to stay."

Kevin took a deep breath. He didn't know how to respond. On one hand, he couldn't stay here if Haven was here. Kevin couldn't breathe with him around. On the other hand, goddamn. Jericho was captivating.

Tanner appeared, saving Kevin from having to decide. "Hey, guys. We're heading to Vegas as soon as Henry can get something set up with our pilot."

Jericho blinked as if coming out of a spell. He looked Tanner's way, but he didn't release Kevin's wrist. "Are Toby and Loyal finally done being dumb?"

Tanner nodded. "Yep. Tucker and Orion are meeting us there in the morning. Are you two up for the trip?"

Kevin tried keeping up. "I'm sorry. What?"

Tanner answered, as if he hadn't misspoken in any way. "Toby and Loyal are eloping. We're all going. We would love for you to join us. There's plenty of room on the plane."

"Oh." That was all Kevin had. He was slow on the uptake, but he definitely realized Tanner was only being nice. "It's okay. I get that's a family thing."

A flash of irritation crossed Tanner's features. He was always serious. "We would like for you to come."

Before he could argue, Jericho spoke up, sounding uncomfortable. "As much as I hate myself for even having to say this, I'll have to check my account. Loyal's medical bills are costing me every extra dime right now. A spur of the moment trip to Vegas isn't really within my budget."

"We intend to fly you there and back. Don't worry over the money. We'll take care of you."

Jericho looked so uncomfortable that Kevin couldn't take it. "You can sleep in my room. That way, I won't feel guilty for crashing a family event and you don't have to feel pressured to spend money you don't have. There's no way you're missing your son's wedding." Not on Kevin's watch.

Tanner nodded. "See. We'll make sure you're good. I have to smother this grill and pack up all the food we made. You two should run home and grab some extra clothes."

"I've been drinking," Jericho muttered under his breath—like he was burdening everyone tonight.

"I'll take you home so you can do what you need."

Jericho looked like Kevin was too good to be true. "Don't you have to grab some stuff too?"

Kevin shook his head. "I travel a few days a week for work more often that I'd like. Sometimes, I have to go at the drop of a hat, so I won't miss a sale. I keep a bag packed in my car. There's nothing standing in the way of us doing what you need to do so you can go see your son get married."

"You're amazing. Thank you." Jericho sounded awed and relieved—like Kevin had truly rescued him.

For the first time in a long time, Kevin felt like he

was good. To anyone else, that might sound ridiculous, but Haven had groomed him to be a good boy, and then treated him like he was bad. Jericho was the first person to look at him like Kevin had needed Haven to look at him since Kevin's heart had given out. Some fucked up things cut too deeply to heal. It was nice, being praised. It was terrifying how far he would go to feel this way a little longer.

TWO

KEVIN HAD BEEN beyond good to Jericho. Jericho had never met anyone who excelled at making him feel as comfortable as Kevin had in the last twenty-four hours. Under any other circumstances, Jericho would have felt guilty as hell over the way Kevin took care of everything. After driving Jericho home so he could shower and pack, Kevin had gotten Jericho something to eat before heading back to Toby's so they could leave for Vegas. When Jericho offered to pay back Kevin's kindness, Kevin had programmed his number into Jericho's phone and said they would figure out something. Kevin's willingness to let Jericho try to make them even was exactly what Jericho needed to relax.

It helped a lot that Kevin smelled like heaven.

Jericho kept moving closer all night without thought, until he half expected Kevin to ask for space. That was how they ended up lounging on the same hotel bed after the wedding. Jericho was simply incapable of giving the man space.

"Toby is really amazing, isn't he? The way he stayed on one knee the whole time, so he wasn't hovering over Loyal while they exchanged vows. That was moving. He really loves your son."

Kevin said everything Jericho had been thinking all night. "They're meant to be. I've always believed that. You have no idea how glad I am they're finally married. They've been through so much. It's time for them to have some happiness." It was so odd. The way Kevin held eye contact and his expressions gave away his every thought—like he was truly invested in their conversation—made Jericho feel as if they had known each other forever. He wanted to keep talking. Jericho genuinely cared about Kevin's life story. He didn't want to go to sleep until he knew everything about the man.

Kevin smiled like a funny thought had hit him. "What will you do with yourself now? This night marks the beginning of the second half of your life. You could do anything."

"Wow. I feel so old," Jericho admitted with a

laugh. "Hmmm. Confession time." Jericho winced as he told on himself. "I asked Toby to add me to his website, so it looks like I'll be going on dates for the first time in at least seventeen years. Jesus."

"Seventeen years. Wow. Are you scared?"

Since Kevin sounded truly interested, Jericho heard himself being honest. "I'm fucking terrified. I got married the day after I graduated from high school, because Loyal's mom was pregnant with him, and her dad was a preacher." Jericho's smile slipped away. "That probably should've been my first clue she wasn't the rebellious daughter she'd always pretended to be. Instead, she was a fucking monster." With his bottom lip held between his teeth, Jericho stared at the wall and willed himself to be quiet. Kevin was a little too easy to talk to.

When Kevin spoke, he sounded hesitant, as if he was used to being chastised for asking questions. "Is her being a monster the reason you haven't dated in so long?"

Damn. He really liked Kevin. There was something about him. He was brave and Jericho couldn't pinpoint exactly why he was so sure of that fact. "Pretty much." Jericho couldn't stop there. "She was an abusive mother. Of course, I didn't find that out until I busted her at it. That's how I ended up with custody of Loyal," he explained. "I tried a couple of times to go on dates after we split. Every single time, when they learned I was a single dad, they would get this look. It was like they were less than thrilled and already plotting a way to get rid of Loyal so they could start a new family with me. After two tries, I decided I couldn't risk it. I couldn't take a chance of coming home from work to find Loyal hurt again by someone else." Jericho's throat swelled at the thought. He swallowed and worked up a smile. "So I said fuck it. I put everything into raising Loyal and cut out that part of myself. Then, one day, I woke up old."

Kevin groaned and pressed his face to mattress for a moment—like he was hiding his smile. "Oh, god. Please don't say it like that. I imagine I'm not that much younger than you. You're making me feel hopeless."

There was no way Kevin was anywhere near close to his age. Jericho went first. "I'm forty-five."

For a moment, Kevin's gaze moved over Jericho's face, as if searching for signs of the passage of time. "Thirty-seven."

"Shut the fuck up," Jericho said, swatting his arm without thought. "You are not."

"Swear to god," Kevin said, digging out his wallet and passing it Jericho's way.

Jericho flipped it open. "Hmmm. Let's see here, Kevin Abbot of 3490 Lake Cove Drive. It seems you are indeed thirty-seven." He dropped the wallet between them. "How is that possible? You look so much younger than me."

Kevin shrugged. "I feel like I'm a hundred and ten." He toyed with the wallet, looking uncomfortable as he stared at the leather piece between them. "So." Kevin cleared his throat. "You've been married since the day after high school and haven't really dated since." His gaze moved Jericho's way. Jericho stopped breathing as he realized how truly gorgeous Kevin was. "Will working for Toby be the first time you've dated men?"

Jericho fought a blush and a guilty smile. "Yep." A terrible thought hit Jericho and he rushed to clear away any confusion. "I'm not trying to take advantage of anyone or mislead them. I don't really know what I'm trying to say. Like, I'm not baiting anyone. If that makes sense?" Jericho was explaining himself badly. The last thing he wanted was for Kevin to think he had zero interest in men and was simply exploiting an opportunity, even though it was only business. "I've had more than seventeen years of keeping myself satisfied with fantasies and that's taught me a lot about myself." Jericho covered his face with both hands and prayed for the floor to open up and swallow him whole. He was beyond humiliated.

"Your ears are red. It's adorable."

Jericho dropped his hands at Kevin's claim. Despite his words, Kevin looked completely calm and collected. His lack of humor eased the embarrassment a bit. Jericho still found it hard to look directly at Kevin after his horrifying confession. "I'm not starting from nothing," Jericho muttered. "Or maybe I am. I don't know."

Kevin nodded. He looked understanding. "At some point, I've hired all three of the Kodiak brothers to go on dates to different events with me. Escort dating is just business. You don't have to explain anything."

An uncomfortable-sounding laugh escaped Jericho. "Be that as it may, I would feel a lot better if you confessed something embarrassing. It feels like I've done everything possible to ensure you never speak to me again after tonight, and I'm sober now. I can't even blame alcohol. It's possible I won't be very good at this escort thing. I'm not very sophisticated."

"My ex is a monster too, and now I'm completely terrified to let anyone else in my space. That's why I hire escorts to go places with me. I don't like always being alone, but I know they won't try to touch me. You haven't said or done a single thing that would make me not want to speak to you again. I like you a lot."

Despite Kevin's admission about liking Jericho, every ounce of discomfort washed away from Jericho's mood, and was replaced with rage. "Are you talking about Haven?" If he learned that asshole had laid a finger on Kevin, Jericho would rip out his spine... if he could find it.

Kevin nodded. He sat up fast, turning his back on Jericho, as if he hated how much he had shown of his heart. "I need to take these contacts out. My eyes are killing me."

Before Jericho could think of anything to say to stop Kevin from running away, his stomach growled. It sounded ridiculously loud in the otherwise quiet room. He pressed a hand to his abdomen. "Wow. That was obnoxious, sir. Calm down in there." His eyes moved to clock beside the bed. "Holy shit. Is that the time? Do you realize we've been talking all night?"

Kevin chuckled as he dug through his bag. "It's

been nice. Once I get these contacts out, we can see what room service has to offer, if you're interested. I'm starving."

"Sounds good," Jericho said, rolling to his feet. He found his bag and peeled off his shirt. Now that he realized they hadn't moved in hours, he felt a bit gross.

"I try not to eat a ton of junk food, but we could order—"

Jericho turned when Kevin suddenly stopped talking mid-speech. A pair of dark framed glasses sat perched on Kevin's nose. They did nothing to hide his gorgeous blue eyes. His gaze was locked on Jericho's bare chest.

Kevin cleared his throat. His chin shot up, as if he forced himself to look away. "We could order an Uber and I could take you out for breakfast. There's a great greasy spoon type place a few miles from the strip."

Someone tried coming in the room, but the privacy lock stopped them. They knocked. "Housekeeping."

"I'll get that," Kevin said, motioning absently toward the door. "Since you're not..." He waved at Jericho's chest. "Yeah." Kevin turned away and headed for the door.

Jericho's eyes lowered. He watched Kevin's ass as he crossed the room. It was like he was losing his mind. Loyal had gotten married and now Jericho couldn't stop eyeing Kevin like the guy would be his next meal. Surely he hadn't been counting the days until he was free to meet someone. After all, it wasn't like Loyal just turned eighteen and moved out. His son was in his twenties. Jericho could have tried dating again sooner. If Kevin thought about it, he would realize that not dating for Loyal's sake couldn't be Jericho's whole story. Fuck. Kevin was sexy as hell in those glasses. How could Mister or Haven or whatever his name was be so damn dumb? How could he be so cruel? Kevin was amazing. Jericho couldn't stop watching his every move. He was so turned on, it hurt. Those fucking glasses. It was like Kevin's sexiness level tripled the moment he set them on his face. Jericho couldn't even explain it. He had never considered himself a pro or con glasses kind of guy.

Without a single thought, Jericho's feet started moving in Kevin's direction as Kevin turned away the maid. Kevin locked the door again. Jericho kept heading his way, as if trapped on autopilot. Kevin turned and froze. Jericho wondered if he looked as intense as he felt. For half a second, Kevin appeared ready to bolt. Then, Kevin's shoulders squared, as if ready for anything Jericho threw his way. Jericho smirked. There was that bravery Jericho couldn't resist. Without a single qualm, Jericho crowded Kevin's space. It was unusual for anyone to be the same height as him, but Kevin matched him in every way. Jericho didn't have to risk a cramp in his neck to press his lips to Kevin's. He didn't try for more than a kiss. Now that he was in Kevin's space, Jericho didn't feel quite as confident. It had been a really long time since he kissed anyone. It was possible he wasn't very good at it any longer. He used to love kissing and he had missed it, but this was his first official kiss with a man. At the exact moment he decided to back down, Kevin's arms encircled him and pulled him closer. Their bodies met. Kevin took control, leaving Jericho free to stop thinking.

In a flash of motion, Jericho found his back against the door. Kevin came at him hard, biting and sucking. Jericho was a mess of need and want. He couldn't focus. Not once in his life had he felt so much passion. He couldn't do anything but hold on as Kevin kneaded his ass, pulling him closer and rocking against him. Jericho worried he might come in his jeans. Kevin was everywhere, biting at his skin and sucking on his neck before returning to his mouth. His tongue stroked Jericho's, stealing his soul. Realistically, he knew he should have been completely terrified. No other man had ever touched Jericho, but this was right. The all-consuming passion was exactly what he needed—what he had been missing for years. Jericho wanted to feel Kevin's skin against his. He tried stealing Kevin's shirt.

"No," Kevin growled against lips. He leaned away and met Jericho's stare. His eyes were so intense that Jericho couldn't draw a full breath. "You're about to come on this shirt so I can take a piece of you home with me. Understood?"

Jericho hadn't expected this. He never dreamed Kevin would be domineering. Goddamn, he wanted it. "Yes."

Kevin tore at the front of Jericho's jeans. "I swear I'll take you to bed, but I need to see. I want to see you."

Even though he was out of practice, this was so much hotter and intense than he had fantasized it would be. At this rate, Jericho would blow the second Kevin touched his dick. All he could do was lean against the door and pray for strength. Jericho had nothing else left to him.

REALISTICALLY, KEVIN RECOGNIZED HE WAS acting like a crazy person. He knew his actions made him look as if he hadn't had sex in ages and was now desperate for Jericho's dick. The thing was, Kevin did feel a certain level of madness for Jericho's cock. He wanted the man's erection filling his hand and body. It had been too long since anyone made him feel anything. All he had known for longer than was healthy was the choking pain of losing Haven coupled with guilt for missing him. Haven was a terrible person. He had broken Kevin and Kevin's hatred grew every day he didn't heal. But Kevin didn't feel any of that right now. All he felt was a burning need in his gut.

Calm settled over Kevin as Jericho's erection sprang from his jeans. Jesus. His crown was soaked with pre-cum already, proving how badly he wanted Kevin. He felt powerful in that moment. Desired. Kevin had to know how Jericho's erection felt pressed against his dick. While staring down between their bodies, Kevin unzipped his pants and pulled out his cock. He brushed his erection down Jericho's length. A sound—like pure lust— filled the air, dragging Kevin's gaze away from the way their cocks played to Jericho's face. His cheeks were flushed, and his eyes were unfocused. Jericho's lips were parted on a pant. He looked so turned on that Kevin had to lock his knees to keep them from buckling. It had been so goddamn long since anyone looked at him like Jericho was now. Something inside Kevin fell away. He swore he felt his walls crumble. Everything he had built to keep his heart safe since Haven broke it disappeared as he stared at Jericho. Maybe he was a mess. Possibly Jericho would never want more than this. None of that mattered. Kevin wanted him anyhow.

Without a word, Kevin leaned in and touched his lips to Jericho's. The crazed kiss from earlier was gone. This was different. Kevin kissed Jericho with sweet hope. He hadn't expected to ever feel that four-letter bastard again. In fact, he hadn't experienced an ounce of expectations of happiness in ages. Then Jericho had come along. Fuck. He wanted everything again. His needy heart couldn't stop begging for abuse.

Kevin leaned away just enough to catch another glimpse of Jericho's open desire. "Strip and get on the bed." The growled words didn't even sound like him. Kevin was someone new with Jericho. Someone stronger.

A small-sounding whimper escaped Jericho, but he did as told. Kevin ate Jericho alive with his stare while Jericho stripped. The man had those sexy dimples right above his ass. Kevin pressed a hand to his stomach at the sight. Jericho was fucking delicious. As Jericho climbed onto the bed, Kevin fought the urge to sink his teeth into Jericho's ass. It was almost scary how badly Kevin wanted him.

Kevin pushed his jeans down his hips as he followed behind him. "I don't suppose you have a condom?"

Jericho shook his head. "No reason to carry one in ages."

A smile that felt wicked, even to Kevin, pulled at his lips. "I guess you really will be coming on my shirt." Jericho's erection twitched at Kevin's remark, making Kevin's smile grow. He would make Jericho scream.

Kevin peeled off his shirt but held on to it. They would need it soon. Kevin hadn't been lying about taking Jericho's cum home. Jericho watched his every move with his bottom lip between his teeth, making Kevin hotter by the second. He had beautiful eyes. They weren't exactly like his son's. They weren't an odd mixture of blue and green. Jericho's were solidly blue, but it was an unusual variation Kevin had never seen before. They were dark—like an Egyptian blue. Beautiful. Kevin held Jericho's stare as he crawled onto the foot of the bed and up Jericho's body. He paused long enough to kiss Jericho's hip before straddling him. A pant escaped Jericho as their erections brushed. Kevin's stomach muscles tightened at the sound. He couldn't recall the last time anyone had made him feel so desired. It was addictive. Maybe they were nothing more than two lonely souls trapped in the same hotel room. Maybe they were more. Either way, Kevin needed Jericho.

Kevin's hips automatically rolled as he claimed Jericho's mouth. They both went all in, immediately doing their best to taste each other's tongues. Kevin rocked against Jericho, taking his pleasure. It wasn't enough. He reached between them and held his cock against Jericho's as he thrust. A moan vibrated through their kiss. Kevin's mind screamed for him to go hard and fast. He wanted to come all over Jericho's pretty dick. Kevin forced himself to go slow. He fully recognized that Jericho might get home to Texas tomorrow, realize he had truly made love to a man, and regret him. Right now, Jericho was turned on and seeking relief. Tomorrow, he might hate himself. Kevin wanted Jericho to remember him with a smile, even if he was never willing to try again.

Pressure climbed up his shaft. The way Jericho felt beneath his lips and between his thighs was amazing. He missed the pressure of lips on his skin. Kevin longed for the breathless moments when a shared orgasm made everything else disappear. There was no one here, making him wait to come. No one demanded he do things a certain way. He was free to kiss and stroke. Kevin could please Jericho and himself in any way he chose without the pressure of following orders. Being with Jericho was like breathing free air.

Hot cum hit him in the chest and a growl vibrated through their kiss, making Kevin realize Jericho came without any warning. Kevin lost his breath. He never expected someone else's orgasm to hit him so hard. He was the reason Jericho shook with pleasure. Kevin had done that. He had made another man happy and it hadn't cost him an ounce of lost dignity. His soul was still intact. Goddamn. Kevin stared down at Jericho in awe. His heart needed more of Jericho's pleasure. Even as he gasped and rode the waves of ecstasy to orgasm, Kevin recognized something beautiful had just happened. He had found himself again, and nothing about him was the same as the version he had left behind with Haven. Thank god.

THREE

FOR THE THIRD time in the past hour, Kevin covered his face with both hands as heat unexpectedly exploded in his cheeks. He couldn't stop thinking about Jericho... or smiling. Wow. Kevin had never acted like he did with Jericho with any other man. In the past, he had always been passive and did as told. Possibly it had something to do with knowing Jericho had never been with another man. Add in the fact he hadn't been with anyone at all in years, and Jericho had the secret combination to opening Kevin's domineering closet. One second, he had watched Jericho cross the room, looking determined. Terror had owned his heart. The next second, their lips had met. Kevin swore he felt Jericho's fear like a living thing. Something inside him snapped. In an instant, he had known exactly what to do. Kevin had known how to fix it. He couldn't let Jericho get away.

Kevin had been so ready to never date again. His mind had been solidly set. Then, Jericho had talked him through a bad heart moment. He had stayed, obviously determined to watch after Kevin's health. Then, Jericho had confessed his secrets while blushing and brought Kevin back to life with his kiss. Kevin hadn't been this obsessed with anything or anyone in a long time. They had a kinship. Kevin hadn't thought he would ever connect with anyone again. It was crazy and sudden. He was scared shitless. It felt good. He felt alive.

Kevin's cellphone rang, pulling him from his musings. Jericho's name stared up at him from the device. He bit his lip, trying to hide his out-of-control smile even though he was alone in his office. Gah. He was so fucked. Kevin tapped the face of the device to answer and set it to speaker phone.

"Hello?"

"Hey." Damn, that was the sexiest "hey" Kevin had ever heard in his life.

Kevin stopped trying to fight his smile. "How are you today?"

"Good," Jericho answered, sounding like he was smiling too. "And you?"

"I'm good. Are you at work?" Jesus. Kevin didn't know what else to talk about.

"No. I work a weird schedule. Usually, it's twenty-four hours on and then two days off. What about you? Are you busy selling all the houses?"

"You could say that. At the moment, I'm playing phone tag with a seller, hoping they'll take my client's offer."

"Oh," Jericho said, sounding disappointed. "Do I need to let you go so your line is free?"

Kevin rushed to keep Jericho on the phone. "No. He'll call the office landline. Very few people have the number to my personal cellphone."

"So I'm special," Jericho said, sounding wicked.

Even though Jericho's claim hadn't been a question, Kevin didn't miss his chance. "You definitely are."

A sexy chuckle rumbled through the line. The sound had goosebumps skirting across Kevin's skin. "In that case, you should let me take you to dinner."

Kevin wasn't missing his chance. "Name the place and I'll be there."

"Nope," Jericho said, sounding determined. "This is a real date. The kind where I pick you up, I take you somewhere nice, and pay. Then, we drive around, while trying to figure out what adults do these days for fun. Eventually, we give up and I drive you home. That's when I walk you to the door and try to steal a kiss."

By the end of Jericho's speech, Kevin was smiling so hard, his cheeks ached. "Sounds like the perfect night."

"What time should I pick you up?"

"How does seven sound?"

Jericho didn't miss a beat. "Sounds great. Text me your address and I'll be there."

"I can't wait." Kevin had never meant anything more.

"See you later, sexy."

"See you," Kevin said, disconnecting their call. He leaned forward and set his crossed arms on the desk before resting his chin on his arms. Kevin stared at his phone, trying to cling to the last wisps of Jericho. He was in so much trouble with this one. Even though Jericho was older than him, he was gorgeous and desirable. People probably tried to win him all the time. He had been married to a woman. Kevin didn't actually know anything about competing with women for a man's attention. Life was a little harder and a lot less free when dating the same sex. Not to mention, Jericho was a fireman. That was a manly job. His co-workers probably would turn cold if they knew. This was new and uncomfortable territory for Kevin. He didn't know where he stood. But for the first time in a long time, Kevin wanted to try. Kevin wanted to take a risk. He couldn't wait to see what happened next, even if it broke him. That was the most terrifying part of all. He was ready for Jericho to demolish him, yet Kevin still hoped he wouldn't. Either way, he still had hope, and that was new.

KEVIN'S HOUSE WAS BADASS. JERICHO MIGHT have been intimidated if his son hadn't just married a millionaire. The Kodiak brothers were proof that not all rich people were boujee. Even though this was his first time at Kevin's place, Jericho felt like he knew Kevin. Kevin had money, but that wasn't what drove him. His large bank account was just part of his life. Jericho wanted to be part of his life too. He took a breath and opened his truck door. Kevin was amazing. He was sexy and sweet. Jericho got the feeling he was lonely—just like Jericho. Jericho could see how someone could feel isolated in this huge house. He eyed the place as he walked to the door. While it wasn't anywhere near as big as Toby's home, the place still screamed money.

Kevin had told him to come to the back door, giving Jericho a good look at the back yard. There was a fire pit on a raised platform surrounded by a circular bench that was the perfect place to enjoy the view of the lake. The pit sat like an island in the center of the pool. The only way to reach it was to swim or walk across a bridge over the water. The pool was a work of art. It wound around the back of the house like a river before disappearing inside the house. Jericho couldn't wait to see what the inside half looked like. The back door of the large two-story home opened before Jericho could knock. The sight of Kevin killed any curiosity Jericho had to see the rest of the house. All Jericho's eyes craved now was the vision currently holding open the back door. He was smiling, but he looked shy. Jericho fought a wave of possessiveness. He truly was enamored. Kevin was Jericho's bear, even if Kevin didn't realize it yet.

"I'd plan to say you have a gorgeous home, but then you opened the door and I caught sight of something even more stunning. Now I can't see anything else." To Jericho's horror, heat exploded through his face the moment he stopped speaking.

"Sorry. Something about you makes me say every thought in my head, and I'm pretty sure I just end up coming across as an idiot." He snapped his teeth together, trying to make the words stop.

Kevin's smile brightened by the second until he laughed. "I think you're adorable." He snagged Jericho's shirttail and hauled him inside. "You smell delicious." Once again, Jericho found his back against a closed door. He went hard at just the thought of what happened last time as Kevin crowded his space. "I thought about you a lot today."

The confession had Jericho's heart speeding. "Good things, I hope."

Kevin brushed the back of his knuckles down Jericho's jaw. His eyes followed the motion. "The best." His gaze moved to Jericho's and held his stare. "But mostly, I just couldn't wait to kiss you again."

"Please?" Jericho couldn't stop the plea from escaping. There wasn't much he would beg for in life. It seemed Kevin's kisses were on that list. The word barely left his lips before Kevin was there. His tongue stroked Jericho's, making Jericho crave feeling what else that tongue could do. Kevin pushed Jericho's shirt up. Cool air brushed his stomach while Kevin massaged his sides. Things turned heated fast. As much as Jericho wanted this,

35

his heart needed to ensure Kevin was cared for first.

He cupped Kevin's face, taking control, and deepening their kiss before pulling away. "I promised to take you to dinner."

Kevin looked sexy and turned on. "Is that really what you want?"

Jericho fought a whimper. He couldn't back down on this. Kevin mattered to him. "Yes. I want to show you off to the world and make sure your needs are met. You need to eat."

For a second, Kevin simply stared at Jericho like he didn't know how to react. Then he shifted uncomfortably and looked away. "Um, I have to be honest. I half expected you to be embarrassed to take me out."

A shot of outrage hit Jericho in the chest. He refused to show it. Kevin looked too sad. Jericho kept his voice calm and even. "Why would I be ashamed?"

With his gaze still averted, Kevin shrugged. "You've never dated a man."

Despite the situation, Jericho smiled. Kevin was adorable. "Since the moment we met, I've felt like I've known you forever. I guess that's why I assumed you knew I don't give a fuck what anyone thinks."

Kevin's gaze slid back Jericho's way. He didn't look away again—like he hung on every word. "You're the person I want to take to dinner tonight. I like you. A lot."

"I like you too." Kevin's quietly spoken confession stole Jericho's breath. It sounded more like a vow than an admission. Kevin took a step closer, pressing Jericho even closer to the door and leaving him nowhere to go. "A lot," Kevin added, making it even harder for Jericho to breathe. "I'd love to go to dinner so everyone can see I'm with the sexiest guy in town and be jealous. But afterward, we're skipping the part where we drive around trying to figure out what people our age do for fun. I know exactly what people our age do, and I'm impatient to be straddling your hips."

Goddamn. Jericho couldn't get enough of Kevin's intensity. No one knew. Nobody understood. He had been alone and craving for so fucking long. Someone like Kevin, someone who looked at Jericho like he would be the man's next meal; that was addictive and everything Jericho had been missing in life. "Deal." In fact, he couldn't wait.

DINNER WITH JERICHO WAS NICE. HE DIDN'T TRY to order for Kevin or even sway him in a certain direction. They decided together where to eat, discussed every item on the menu, and picked different meals so they could try each other's food. Just as it had been in Vegas, Jericho talked almost nonstop. Kevin never tired of hearing his voice or watching him smile as he spoke. His eyes shone bright with an inner beauty that kept Kevin mesmerized. It was obvious Jericho had found a certain happiness in being alone. He didn't need anyone, and it was refreshing. It was funny how Jericho's lack of neediness made Kevin want him to find Kevin necessary.

"How long have you lived here?" Jericho asked as Kevin pointed him to a spot in the garage to park his truck.

"Almost two years."

Jericho showed his first hint of discomfort all night. He rubbed the back of his neck as they slid from the truck and headed for the door. "I guess my tiny house in the middle of nowhere must seem..."

Kevin looked his way when Jericho didn't finish his thought. "Seem what?"

Jericho shrugged. "Small, I guess."

At Jericho's response, Kevin froze with the door

halfway open. "Do you honestly think I'm the kind of person who cares about the size of someone's house?"

A huge smile sprang to Jericho's lips, lighting his whole face. "You're a real estate agent. I imagine you immediately start assessing the worth of someone's house the minute you step inside the same way I spot all the fire hazards."

A chuckle escaped Kevin. "True, but I've only been to your house twice, and—to be honest—I didn't really look away from you the entire time we were there." Jericho's expression—like Kevin made him happy—had Kevin taking his hand and leading him through the house. As Kevin cleared his bedroom door with Jericho in tow, he slowed. For the first time in a long time, he really looked at the space where he slept each night. Kevin's gaze skirted the room, trying to see things through Jericho's eyes. It wasn't that hard to imagine Jericho's thoughts. He had once been just like Jericho—out of his depth. Too late, he realized his room was filled with fetish decor. Nothing bawdy, but there were some things that were unmistakably meant for bondage play. "I'll have all this shit removed before you come back. I should've gotten rid of all this BDSM bullshit a long time ago. It just sort of moved with me from New

Braunfels when I left Haven, and I don't know why."

"Don't worry about me," Jericho said, sounding completely comfortable. "This is your bedroom. You should be allowed to do whatever."

A bitter smile touched Kevin's lips. He sat on the edge of his bed and eyed all the playthings he had allowed Haven to bring into his life and he had somehow ended up with. "These things aren't me. Not anymore. When I was with Haven, I was different. I let him change me." Kevin hated himself for bringing up Haven now, but he had to explain. "He fed me a lot of bullshit about how much trust there is in complete surrender, as if the dependence ran both ways. As if we were equal when I was helpless. I ate that shit up for every meal, and I let it..." Kevin didn't know how to finish that sentence. He had let Haven break him, but he didn't know how to admit that. Kevin cleared his throat and flashed Jericho a smile. "I shouldn't be talking about him with you. If you give me another chance, this stuff will be gone next time and I won't say his name again. Promise."

Jericho's serious expression never wavered as he closed the distance between them. He kept moving until he stood between Kevin's knees. Jericho ran his hands up Kevin's thighs while holding his stare. "If someone has to change you before they can love you, then it's not you they want. You deserve someone who can't get enough of you exactly as you are. Someone who'll take whatever dish you serve as long as it comes from you. Keep your toys or get rid of them. I don't care. As long as you keep inviting me back, I'll come. No matter what. You don't have to change for me."

Kevin's hands found Jericho's ass. He hauled him closer. Hunger clawed at his gut. "What about you? Have you ever been at anyone's mercy? Hands bound. Forced to endure whatever pleasure they pull from you. Has anyone ever made you beg while there's nothing you can do but take it?"

"No." Jericho looked and sounded so turned on that Kevin couldn't stop.

"Then I guess I get to be your first."

"Seems fair," Jericho said, moving in for a kiss. "You've been a first for me in a lot of ways."

Kevin used his size against Jericho and towed him into bed. With a tuck and a roll, he had Jericho trapped beneath him. He tore at Jericho's clothes, uncaring if he moved too fast. Jericho was amazing. Kevin wanted him. Something inside him solidified with every stroke of tongue and lost article of clothing. Kevin craved the control Jericho freely allowed. His body burned to take what he wanted how he wanted. Without thought, he found himself strapping Jericho's wrists into the Velcro cuffs attached to his headboard. They had been there so long, Kevin had forgotten about them until he put them to use. Beyond the occasional moan, Jericho didn't make a sound. He let Kevin have his way. It was the most empowering experience of Kevin's life. At the same time, Kevin recognized Jericho owned him in that moment unlike anyone ever had. Kevin would have given Jericho anything he requested. As he licked a path down Jericho's nude body, Kevin was lost.

Kevin stroked himself as he swallowed Jericho's cock. The cry that rent the air had Kevin putting his heart into blowing Jericho. His throat tightened around the man's dick before he forced himself to slow. Things were different tonight. Kevin had protection. Hell would freeze before Kevin missed his chance at riding Jericho.

A cry of denial escaped Jericho as Kevin gave him one last lick and moved away. Jericho writhed, straining against his restraints. An evil smile pulled at Kevin's lips as he found the lube and ripped open a condom.

"You even look like a man set on tormenting me."

Kevin rolled the condom down Jericho's length. "No. I'm just picturing the way this sexy dick is about to stretch me wide." He held Jericho's stare. "I can't fucking wait."

Jericho released a loud pant. Pre-cum leaked from Kevin's cock at the sight of Jericho's open lust. He quickly coated the sheath with lube and tossed a leg over Jericho's body. Kevin's patience was gone. It had been too long since anything other than toys filled his ass. He needed the real thing. Jericho felt like the realest thing Kevin ever encountered in every way.

Kevin fisted Jericho's erection and held him in place as he lowered himself onto Jericho's cock. His eyes fell closed as his asshole stretched, giving way to the intrusion.

"Fuck. Oh, fuck." Jericho's words sounded winded—like he had already run a marathon. Kevin tugged at his dick, seeking relief.

Jericho moaned. "Goddamn. You're so sexy. Yes. Do that. I want to watch you play with yourself."

Without an ounce of hesitation, Kevin took what he wanted even as he gave Jericho his way. He lifted and sat, riding Jericho's dick at the perfect angle while pulling at his cock. Kevin fucked his hand and

Jericho while Jericho strained beneath him. Kevin couldn't look away. He was in the zone. He felt powerful and sexy with Jericho between his thighs, writhing while watching Kevin jack off and use his body. In a detached way, he wondered if Jericho was disappointed with the lack of foreplay. Yet, Kevin couldn't slow down. He needed to blow cum all over Jericho's body. Kevin had to see Jericho covered in their combined ejaculant.

Kevin threw his head back and strained, thrusting hard into his fist while grinding down on Jericho's dick. Pressure beat at his crown, begging for release. He was right there, poised on the edge. A cry bounced from the walls, assaulting his ears. Jericho stiffened between his thighs. An orgasm ripped from Kevin. His entire body drew up tight before shaking in release. He moaned and babbled as he stroked out every wave he could get while his ass sucked Jericho deeper. Kevin felt whole. For the first time in more years that he could recall, everything felt right. There was no pride or shame. Only beauty existed in that moment. Jericho was exactly what Kevin needed. He had to hang on to him for as long as Jericho would allow. There were no other options to his mind.

———

JERICHO HADN'T EXPECTED THINGS TO BE SO intense. Everything with Kevin felt twice as powerful than they had ever been with anyone else. Every few seconds, Kevin's lips skimmed Jericho's throat. Jericho's heart ate every kiss alive. He had been alone for so damn long. Jericho was starved for affection. It had been a long day and Jericho should have been tired. He was too happy to sleep. For too many years to count, Jericho had been going through the motions with nothing to look forward to. Before Kevin, his life had been relatively empty.

His wrists were sore from straining against the restraints. Jericho fought the urge to cover his face. He had never let anyone bind him. This man had cuffs built into his headboard. Jericho was so out of his depth and loving it. Being with Kevin was exhilarating. He didn't want to be anywhere else.

"When we were talking in Vegas, you said you had a lot of time to figure some things out about yourself since you've been single for so long. What did you figure out?"

Jericho smiled into the dark. Kevin sounded uncomfortable—like there was more to his question but he didn't know how to ask. He understood what

Kevin was getting at. Kevin wanted to know if this was an experiment on Jericho's part. Jericho started the best place he could. "When I was kid, I had this friend, David. We did everything together. He lived on the same street and if I wasn't at his house, he was at mine. Then, in the ninth grade, he got his first girlfriend. The next thing I knew, he did everything with her and I was only his backup plan if she was busy. I was bitterly jealous. So much so, that my mom had to step in and talk to me about growing up and growing apart. She reassured me that it happened to everyone eventually and I would meet someone who made me feel the same about my friends. She said I would understand when it happened to me. Then I met Loyal's mom, Amelia. I never felt the way my mom described. Obviously, I loved her, but she never made me want to shut everyone else out. I wasn't willing to give up everyone for her." Jericho knew he wasn't doing a great job of explaining himself, but he kept talking, hoping Kevin would understand he hadn't always known himself.

"After Amelia was gone and I'd been single for a while, I started looking harder at myself. I realized I never really thought about a person's sex when I checked them out on the sly. It never

occurred to me that wasn't how everyone else felt until I met this trans woman at the gym. She said she had to change at home before and after her workout, because some of the other women were uncomfortable with her being in the locker room. Later that night, I was telling a guy at work about it, and he got really defensive, saying of course women didn't want some dude in there while they were changing. That really pissed me off." Jericho felt his anger rising all over again—like he was back in the moment he realized not everyone thought like him. "I couldn't believe he didn't realize she was a girl and belonged in the women's locker room. Then, he says, 'Get real, Jericho. That's a dude. Like, what if you took that home and found a dick? You can't seriously tell me you'd still fuck him.' I didn't even hesitate. I was like, yeah, I would still fuck *her*. He kind of smirked and said, 'I hate to be the bearer of bad news, then, but that means you're gay.' I rolled my eyes and blew it off as him being a backwoods ignorant fucker. The more I thought about it, though, the more I recognized he wasn't totally wrong. Maybe I wasn't gay, per se, but neither was I completely straight. I think, looking back on things, I did like David more than a friend should, and—if I was being honest with myself—David wasn't the only man I've ever wanted."

Jericho felt the overwhelming need to be truthful in every way, especially with Kevin staring at him and hanging on every word. "The idea of dating another woman doesn't appeal to me, but I still like women. Straight porn still turns me on, but so does gay porn. I flirt with men equally if not more than I flirt with women. In truth, I'm not bothered if someone is male, female, or transitioning between the two. People's hearts are what get me. If someone is beautiful on the inside, that shit hits me in the chest. Being nice is sexy as hell. There's a lot of confidence in caring about other people in a world this ugly. Loyal's mom was absolutely beautiful on the outside, but she was the ugliest person in the world on the inside. It completely turned me off in every way. Now, meeting someone with a heart of gold is irresistible." Jericho focused on Kevin. The light from inside the bathroom lit up his eyes. "Gets me every time," Jericho added, sounding absent, even to his ears. "You're gorgeous."

"You're too good to be true." Kevin said the words with such surety, even Jericho wondered when the other shoe would drop, and then he was insulted. His affront lasted half a second before

Jericho realized he would have to prove Kevin wrong. Maybe Jericho wasn't the one who cut Kevin, and it wasn't his responsibility to stitch him up, but Jericho still wanted the job.

"You should probably kiss me anyway. Just to be on the safe side."

The way Kevin kissed him without argument gave Jericho hope. Kevin was the first person Jericho had liked in a long time. He didn't want this—whatever it was—to stop. Maybe he was a rescuer at heart. Jericho had always loved helping people. This felt different, though. This felt like Jericho would find the world's greatest prize on the other side of Kevin's walls. He wanted that. And maybe, just maybe, Kevin was the one doing the saving.

FOUR

AN AMAZING NIGHT turned into an awesome morning. Jericho didn't want to return to real life. Tomorrow, he would be back at work and he would be back to worrying what his position was in Kevin's life. Right now, though, with Kevin's hand down the front of his boxer briefs, massaging Jericho's cock while sucking on his neck, Jericho was on cloud nine. At the moment, he knew his place. Soon, it would be inside Kevin.

The doorbell chimed. Kevin groaned. "No. It can't be true. Let's ignore it." The sound cut through the air again. Kevin glanced down at the obvious bulge in his jeans. "Goddamn." He rolled from the bed and tugged on a flannel shirt, ensuring it was long enough to hide his erection before heading for the bedroom door. "Don't move. I'm coming back to finish this."

Jericho took a steadying breath as he watched Kevin cross the room. He wasn't going anywhere... except maybe to grab a drink from the kitchen. It was damn dehydrating being with Kevin.

Jericho slipped from the bed and headed for the hall. He knew he could cut through the bedroom across the hall to get to the kitchen without worrying whoever was at the door would see him. Still, he peeked around the corner to be sure. His trip to the kitchen ended short as he watched Kevin open the door. Haven stood on the other side. Without thought, Jericho backed out of sight. It wasn't truly his intention to eavesdrop. Yet he didn't move away. It went against Jericho's nature to be insecure. He simply couldn't figure out where he stood with Kevin. Jericho wasn't surprised Haven had shown. In truth, he had expected the man sooner. Still, it chafed.

"Haven." The hatred in Kevin's voice couldn't be missed.

"That's not what you used to call me." Even though Jericho couldn't see Haven's face, he could hear the smirk in his voice.

Kevin sounded dead when he next spoke. "Well,

I also used to wet the bed as a kid and call my sister every night before she died. Things change." Jericho made a mental note to ask about Kevin's sister.

"May I come in?" Contrite didn't fit Haven.

Jericho shifted farther out of sight as Kevin stepped back to let Haven inside. No doubt Kevin didn't want his neighbors talking. With Haven hosting BDSM demos to every rich dude for miles, everyone probably knew his face by now. Judging by the way Kevin had reacted to Jericho seeing his bedroom decor, he wouldn't want his neighbors to associate him with Haven's lifestyle.

"What do you want?" Wow. Kevin sounded done.

"Since I can see you're already picturing me being disemboweled, I promise I won't stay long." Damn. That made Jericho wish he could see Kevin's face.

"That's probably best."

Haven got straight to the point. "Toby's husband Loyal gave me some great advice after the last time I saw you. Actually, it was more of a kick in the pants than advice, but still." Jericho strained to hear every word about his son. "Plus, Orion isn't speaking to me now and I didn't realize how much that would hurt." Jericho rolled his eyes. Of course, this visit was for

Haven's peace and not Kevin—the one who deserved it. Jericho fought the urge to burst from his hiding spot—clothed or not, until Haven spoke again. "I'm sorry. This isn't an 'I'm sorry, please take me back.' I'm genuinely really, really sorry for everything I did." Jericho really wanted to know what he had done. "You deserve so much better than you got from me. I took advantage of your heart. Worse than that, I abused your trust. I'm not asking for your forgiveness. I know I'm beyond that. The only reason I'm here is because I need you to know that I fully recognize what I did and what I lost." Haven paused. He sounded truly hurt. Jericho swiped his hand over his eyes. This was a mess. "I hope you find the happiness you deserve and never think of me again."

Jericho shifted positions again, watching as Haven headed for the door. As he touched the doorknob, Kevin spoke up, making Jericho fear he was about to be crushed. They had history. Jericho had nothing.

"Mister." Haven froze with his hand on the knob. His gaze shot Kevin's way at the name. Kevin's voice hardened again. "Don't come back here."

At Kevin's words, Haven gave him a sharp nod and let himself out. Jericho counted to ten. He didn't want to burst into the room and look as crazy as he felt. Instead, he measured each step he took until he closed the distance between them. Kevin hadn't budged from staring at the door. That bothered Jericho more than he wanted to admit. Jericho snagged Kevin's waist and towed him into his arms until his chest cradled Kevin's back. Kevin's body was stiff. Jericho brushed his lips across Kevin's nape. Kevin's muscles relaxed. Goosebumps rose beneath Jericho's lips.

"Are you okay, gorgeous?"

Kevin reached over his shoulder and ran his fingers through Jericho's hair, easing the tightness in Jericho's chest. "Yeah. I'm good."

Jericho's lips moved to Kevin's shoulder. "Good. You should come back to bed."

"Let's grab you something to drink first. Your throat sounds raw and I'm about to make you scream."

Damn. Jericho was onboard with this plan. Whatever had gone on between Haven and Kevin, they were over now. Kevin belonged to Jericho now, and Jericho fully intended to make Kevin happier than he had ever been.

KEVIN EXPECTED A BLACK MOOD TO ENGULF HIM, the way it always did after an encounter with Haven. Instead, he felt nothing. He had a feeling that was thanks to Jericho's presence more than Haven's apology. Jericho's lips brushed his neck again, reminding Kevin he was still standing in the middle of the foyer. He forced himself to move past Haven's surprise visit. His life was headed in a different direction now.

Without a word, he took Jericho's hand and headed for the kitchen. It wasn't until he poured Jericho a glass of mineral water that he realized he should be taking better care of Jericho's health. "Do you have any plans today?"

Jericho smirked. "I thought we did."

His confidence was sexy as hell. "Oh, I haven't forgotten about that. What I meant was, do you have time for me to take you to breakfast first? I haven't been spoiling you like you deserve."

Jericho's features softened. "I don't expect you to spoil me. You do that already by just spending time with me."

Kevin passed the water Jericho's way. "This isn't about expectations. Being with you..." Kevin searched for a way to express his thoughts, "... it's weird for me." That did not come out the way he intended. Kevin rushed to fix it. "I'm not used to making decisions." He growled. Kevin couldn't find the words. Jericho made him want to take control and be the caretaker, but he was used to being told what to do. "Like, I know you know I want you sexually. That's beyond obvious. But I also need for you to understand that I want you fed and hydrated. Your well-being matters. May I take you to breakfast, please?"

Jericho set his glass aside and closed the space between them. He gripped Kevin's hips before slipping his arms around him. His gaze never wavered from holding Kevin's stare. "Short answer, yes. I would love to go to breakfast with you. But I also need to say, I love that you care. Please don't stress about being with me. You don't have to overthink everything with me. I'm a grown man. If I'm thirsty, I can get a drink. Trust me, I'll tell you if I'm hungry. You have no idea how much I love that you care, but I also don't consider it your sole responsibility. You understand we're equals in this thing, right?"

It was odd as hell. They were equals, and the concept was so damn foreign to Kevin that he hadn't even considered it. "Yes." Even Kevin heard the question in his answer.

With a shake of his head, Jericho went to work on the buttons of Kevin's flannel. "Give me twenty minutes and then I promise we'll get breakfast. I'm not ready to share you just yet, but I also need to know your needs are met." His gaze lifted from his task to meet Kevin's stare. "Including your sexual needs." He pushed the shirt down Kevin's arms. "When I saw Haven here earlier, I had a moment of fear that you might choose him. I don't know why. Maybe I feel a little out of my league with you."

It was like Jericho held the secret to making Kevin strong. His words were like a lightning bolt, zapping his confidence back to life. He hauled Jericho against him. Their bare chests met. "Fuck that." Kevin claimed Jericho's mouth with more force than necessary, but he poured his heart into their kiss. No one in their right mind would choose Haven over Jericho. Kevin would never let Jericho feel less than anyone. He knew how that felt. It was a nightmare he wouldn't wish on anyone, especially someone as amazing as Jericho. It was time to put Haven behind him. He would start today.

FIVE

KEVIN: *Do you have any plans tonight?*

Jericho: *No, but I don't get off work until eight.*

Kevin: *Maybe I can bring you dinner when you get home?*

Jericho: *That sounds amazing. If you beat me there, there's a spare key under the flowerpot closest to the new ramp Toby built.*

Kevin: *Wow. I felt the trust in that one.*

Jericho: *You've given me plenty of reasons to believe in you. I also don't have anything to steal. LOL!*

Kevin: *Oh, I don't know. Maybe I'll finger all your underwear before you get home.*

Jericho: *You should wait until I get home and finger the ones I'm wearing.*

Jericho: *I can't believe I sent that text.*

Kevin: *You're adorable.*

Jericho: *I'm a loser.*

Jericho: *I can't believe I sent that text either.*

Kevin: *You're endearing, and I can't wait to get into the underwear you're wearing.*

Jericho: *A GUY AT WORK ASKED WHAT HAPPENED to my wrists. I told him an extremely sexy man tied me to my bed. Oops. Guess I outed myself.*

Kevin: *Is that okay? I know you work with a lot of men's men.*

Jericho: *Of course it's okay. I'm lucky as hell you spend time with me.*

Kevin: *I still can't believe that shirt I used to tie you to the chair left marks on your wrists. I feel terrible about that.*

Kevin: *Also, I'm damn proud every time we're together. We should be together more often.*

Jericho: *Agreed.*

Kevin: *MERRY CHRISTMAS.*

Jericho: *Good morning, sexy. Merry Christmas to you as well.*

Kevin: *I know it's a day for families, but—if you're free—I'd love for you to come by tonight when you're done making the rounds.*

Jericho: *Sounds great. Is seven too early? I don't know what time you celebrate with your family.*

Kevin: *Seven is great. I'll leave the back door unlocked for you.*

Jericho: *I can't wait.*

THE HOUSE WAS DARK AND SILENT AS JERICHO let himself inside. Since the back door was unlocked, he assumed Kevin was home. He followed the sound of crackling until he found Kevin, sitting on the floor next to the Christmas tree and staring at an electric fire. A plain white t-shirt stretched across his back as he brought a coffee cup to his lips. Workout shorts covered his bottom half, making Jericho wonder how long he had been home. Jericho stole a moment to watch him. Kevin was spectacular. It had only been three weeks since they met, and Jericho couldn't shake the feeling Kevin was already under his skin.

After so many years of being single, Jericho fully recognized he should play the field. It wasn't like he planned to remarry or jump into a serious relationship with the first person he met. Yet, Jericho wasn't interested in looking anywhere else. In fact, he found himself comparing everyone to Kevin. They didn't have his soft dark hair or his wide shoulders. Everyone was missing his dark blue eyes and perfect smile. No one else made Jericho's stomach flutter while he babbled in nervousness. All roads led back to Kevin every single time.

Kevin glanced over his shoulder. His eyes lit with happiness when he spotted Jericho. "Hey. I didn't hear you come in." He pushed to his feet and met Jericho halfway. Their lips met before Jericho could respond. Jericho had to take a breath as an intense wave of emotion washed over him. The truth hit him; he didn't want to be anywhere else. He might be in a bit of trouble.

When his eyes opened, he saw his feelings staring back at him. Jericho realized he was happy. For the first time in forever, he was completely happy with exactly where he was in life. He wasn't waiting for the next big moment. Something had changed.

Jericho dragged his gaze down Kevin's body,

giving his eyes a feast. "How long have you been home?"

Kevin shrugged. "All day."

"I thought you were spending the day with your family," Jericho said, switching the gift bag he held from one hand to the other.

A hint of discomfort crossed Kevin's features. "My family celebrates on Christmas Eve, but I haven't been back home in years."

Jericho realized he should have asked more questions sooner. "Where is home?"

"Franklin, Tennessee."

"Oh." Jericho tried to think of a way to learn more without being too intrusive. "That's not horribly far. I mean, flying is a nightmare this time of year, but it's like—what? A thirteen, fourteen-hour drive?"

"I have a gift for you," Kevin said with a bright smile, ignoring Jericho's questions.

Jericho let it go. He knew he was being intrusive. He held out the bag for Kevin. "I have one for you too."

As Kevin accepted the gift, he looked adorably confused—like no one gave him presents. "Thank you." He said the words while staring at the bag in awe.

Suddenly, Jericho wanted to give Kevin the world. While he didn't have Kevin's money, he had heart. He could make this man happy. "Open it." The instant the words left his lips, Jericho's nervous chatter set in. "I had my first job for Cubs for Rent the other night. It had been my plan to make extra money for Loyal's hospital bills, but Toby paid them. So I had a little extra money to get you exactly what I wanted." He pressed his lips together, forcing himself to stop talking as Kevin pulled the watch from inside the bag. He didn't last. "It's a watch that monitors your heart rate and blood pressure. That way, I know you're staying safe. If your heart gets out of whack, it'll beep at you and you'll know to take a breath." He met Kevin's stare. His mouth went dry at Kevin's expression. He looked enthralled. "Promise me you'll take a break if it beeps." He cared. Jericho needed to know Kevin was okay.

"You're amazing. Thank you." Kevin looked genuinely moved. "I love the idea of knowing when I need a break." He flashed Jericho a humorous smile. "I also can't wait to tell people they have to go away from me because they're making my watch beep." A chuckle escaped Jericho at the picture Kevin painted with his claim. Kevin took Jericho's hand and tugged him toward the tree. "You have to come open your gift now."

Jericho was oddly excited. While he had already been spoiled by Loyal this year, he couldn't wait to see what Kevin had done. There was only one gift beneath the tree. It was a gold box about the size of a hardback book. Kevin passed it Jericho's way as they filled the loveseat across from the fireplace. The lid easily lifted from the box without Jericho having to fight with bows or wrapping paper. Two items stared up at him—a small remote on a keychain and a velvet box.

"The remote controls the garage door, back door, and will set or disable the alarm. I figured, since I know where your spare keys are, you should have a way to get into my place too."

Jericho was blown away. He didn't have anything worth stealing, so letting Kevin know where the key was hidden meant nothing. Kevin letting him into this space was a hell of a lot of trust. "Wow. I don't know what to say. I won't let you regret trusting me."

Kevin shrugged. "You're my best friend. If anyone should have a key, it's you."

Jericho's throat swelled. The title was very fitting. Even though he constantly questioned what they were to each other, he knew they were friends before anything else. "Thank you." Even Jericho heard his heart in his voice.

"Open the rest," Kevin urged, looking excited— like he was the one getting the gift.

Jericho focused on the velvet box and flipped it open. It was a gold rope chain with a tiny charm. The charm looked like a series of loops crossing each other. It was gorgeous and looked expensive.

"It's a triquetra," Kevin explained, sounding nervous. "For protection," he added. "Since I always worry when you're on a call."

Jericho met Kevin's gaze. "It's gorgeous. Thank you." His words didn't feel like enough. Jericho needed to say more. "You're amazing. Truly. Meeting you is the best thing that's happened to me in a really long time."

"Same. Will you stay the night?"

Jericho didn't hesitate. "Yes. Will you tell me why you didn't spend the holiday with your parents?"

A small smile touched Kevin's lips. "If you'll let me put the necklace on you."

He passed the velvet box Kevin's way. "Deal."

Kevin took the box and gently tugged the necklace loose. He kept his gaze on his hands as

Jericho leaned closer. Kevin spoke as he worked on the necklace's clasp. "My sister died three years ago. We were really close. Brie was my best friend. I talked to her every single day." Kevin swiped his fingers across Jericho's collar, tracing the line of the necklace as it fell in place. His eyes followed the motion. "She stood behind every choice I made, ready to fight on my behalf whether I was right or not. She's also my biggest failure."

Kevin's claim shocked Jericho into speaking. "Why would you say that?"

A sad smile touched Kevin's lips. He cleared his throat. "Because she was always there, looking out for me. Then she killed herself. Not only do I have no idea why, she never said a thing to make me worry. But now I think, maybe it's because I never asked. She seemed to always have it together. Or maybe I've always been such a mess that she looked great by comparison. Either way, I failed everyone because I didn't save her. It's hard for me to go home. I see her face everywhere but nowhere. It's too hard."

That was horrible, but Jericho couldn't help but to see things from another point of view. "You do realize, though, that your parents have already lost one child and it probably kills them that you're stealing yourself from them too." He immediately regretted saying anything. "Sorry. That was the parent in me speaking." He had almost lost his child recently. Jericho saw everything from that perspective now. He swiped his palms on his thighs and kept diving in. "If you ever decide you want to see them, I'd be happy to go with you, if you think it would help. Otherwise, I promise I'll leave the topic alone."

Kevin's mouth lifted slightly in one corner. "Thank you. I'll think about it."

That was all Jericho could ask. He set the box aside and shifted forward. Jericho kept moving until he straddled Kevin's lap. The happiness in Kevin's eyes kept Jericho transfixed. "I think it's time to make out."

"Is it?" The laughter in Kevin's voice was addicting.

Jericho nodded even as he closed the final gap between them. This was the best Christmas in memory for Jericho. His son was still with him and happily married. He had a sexy man beneath him. His whole damn life felt like a holiday miracle.

Damn, Kevin could practically feel

himself falling for Jericho a little more every single day. He couldn't explain how this happened. All Kevin knew was, he had spent the entire week obsessing over the perfect Christmas gift. He fought the urge to spend an ass ton of money, buying Jericho all the things. Instead, he had gone with understated beauty. The necklace, while relatively plain, was Bulgari and cost forty thousand. He wouldn't be telling Jericho that. Instead, he planned to enjoy draping Jericho in subtly expensive gifts and taking over his life.

Jericho kissed his neck. Kevin tilted his chin back, giving him more access. He breathed through his nose, savoring the building lust. The string of his workout shorts loosened. Jericho's hand slipped inside. Kevin squeezed his eyes closed and savored the moment.

"Tell me what you want?"

A thousand sexual images crammed Kevin's head at the question. He wanted everything with Jericho. One fantasy stood out above the rest. "I want your dick in my mouth."

"Jesus."

A smile that felt evil even to Kevin pulled at his lips at Jericho's breathless curse. He took control, flipping Jericho onto the other side of the loveseat before going on the attack. He tore at Jericho's jeans as he kissed a path down Jericho's body. His knees hit the floor as Jericho's cock sprang from his underwear. Kevin's mouth watered as he stared at Jericho's erection. He dragged out the anticipation. His gaze flipped upward, meeting Jericho's stare. Hunger clawed at his insides. Jericho's face was flushed. He looked at Kevin like he held the key to all happiness for him. Kevin had never felt more empowered by anyone. Reality slammed into Kevin. He had sworn he would never get on his knees for another man. Yet here he was without a single thought. Kevin saw the truth. He might be the one on his knees, but Jericho wasn't in charge. In fact, Jericho looked like he might die if Kevin stopped.

Kevin's throat swelled. Jericho was the good man Kevin deserved. He was worthy of seeing Kevin in this position. "You're beautiful." He hoped Jericho understood he meant on the inside. Jericho was gorgeous on the outside too, but he was good. Kevin needed him.

Jericho's expression softened—like he could read Kevin's heart. He stroked Kevin's jaw. "Let's move this to the bedroom. I need to feel your weight pinning me to the bed."

Kevin's eyes stung as he shifted to his feet. He

was happy. For the first time in years, he felt his heart slowly mending. He swore he could hear the click of the shattered pieces in his chest sliding back into place, becoming whole again. Being with Jericho was beautiful. Kevin wouldn't let him get away.

SIX

KEVIN: *What are your plans for New Years?*

Jericho: *I don't have anything planned. Why?*

Kevin: *I'm thinking I'll go see my parents. Would you like to come? It wouldn't cost you anything but time.*

Jericho: *I would love to go.*

SINCE BARING HIS SOUL ON CHRISTMAS, KEVIN hadn't stopped thinking about Jericho's claim. He didn't want his parents to feel like they had lost two children. He didn't know how to stop other than to just do it. Make the trip. While sitting at the same kitchen table he had eaten at every night growing up and watching his mom exclaim over pictures of Loyal, Kevin was glad he had given in. His parents had hated Haven. From day one, they had side-eyed him and warned Kevin against him at every turn. At the time, he had been outraged by their insults. He couldn't see what they saw. Even now, after everything Haven had done, he still didn't fully understand their distaste. After all, Haven had been nothing but nice to them. But it was funny, they were doting on Jericho like he was a second child. Kevin couldn't stop shaking his head at the oddness of it all.

His mom slapped Jericho's arm, the way she always did when she remembered something important. "We have a timeshare at a cabin in the mountains. In about three weeks, we're headed that way to go skiing. You should talk Kevin into going and bring your son. He's so handsome. I would love to meet him."

Jericho flashed her a grateful smile. "Loyal is in a wheelchair, so he probably won't be skiing anytime soon."

She blushed. "Oh, no. I didn't realize."

"No. Don't worry over it, Minnie," Jericho rushed to reassure her. "You didn't know. As for us, I'd love to go, but I need to look at my schedule. I tend to work twenty-four hours on and forty-eight off, so my workdays are always different."

"Those sound almost like nursing hours. That's what I did before retiring."

Jericho nodded. "I'm a firefighter."

Minnie cackled, making Kevin smile. "You just keep getting hotter by the second."

Heat crawled up Kevin's face. He couldn't believe his mom was flirting with Jericho. Kevin bit the inside of his cheek to keep from laughing. Thankfully, his dad came to the rescue.

"Come see the she-shed I'm building Minnie. It's mostly finished except for a few cosmetic things. You can point out all the fire hazards." He released a loud laugh at his own joke.

"Kevin and I will meet you outside in a minute, Wayne."

Kevin swallowed down a groan at his mother's announcement. It wasn't a save after all. They were conspiring so his mom could talk to him alone. Before his dad could completely get away with Jericho, Kevin snagged Jericho around the waist and stole a kiss. Jericho winked and followed Wayne outside. Kevin stared at the door that stole Jericho, for much longer than necessary.

"Wow, Kev. He's really amazing. And hot."

Kevin tore his gaze away from the door to focus on the blue eyes that looked so much like his. "Yes. He is."

His mom covered her face for a second, barely hiding a blush. "I feel so terrible suggesting a ski trip. You should've warned me his son is in a wheelchair."

"It didn't come up."

As he looked on, his mom chewed her bottom lip. He fought the urge to tell her get on with it. "Are you finished avoiding us now?"

Ah. There it was. "It's not you I've been avoiding, and you know it. How can you keep living here?" Kevin asked before he could stop it from happening. He heard the horror and desperation in his voice, but it was out of his control.

A sad smile touched Minnie's lips. She glanced around the room. Even though this wasn't the room where his sister had been found dead, it was under the same roof. Kevin hated it. "There are more happy memories in this house than not. I think I would feel farther away from Brie than I already do if we moved. We missed you at Christmas."

"I know." The guilt was thick. "It's not easy for me to come here. I see her everywhere." Kevin had to clear his throat. While a lot of people didn't feel close to their siblings, Brie and he had been like best friends from birth. He was five when Brie was born. From the first time he had held her, he loved her. He was supposed to protect her. Still, this was his mom. "But I promise I'll try harder. Jericho almost lost his son earlier this year, and he pointed out how I was stealing two children from you by not coming around, so I'll try."

"I think I'm really going to like this one," Minnie said more for herself. "Trying is all I can ask of you." Minnie pushed from the kitchen table. "Now, we should probably rescue Jericho before your dad has him hanging fixtures or something. You know everyone is free labor to him."

Kevin picked up the pace at the reminder. His dad was likely to put Jericho to work. Kevin didn't want that. Jericho needed to conserve his energy. A smile touched Kevin's lips. He already had a different job planned for Jericho tonight. Damn, he couldn't wait to get to the hotel. He didn't know how much longer he could stay here.

KEVIN'S PARENTS WERE REALLY AMAZING. Jericho was glad Kevin had decided to make the trip. He was proud of Kevin for trying. It also broke his heart to see the pain growing in Kevin's eyes all night. Being here was hard for him. Jericho wanted to make it better.

"I assume y'all are staying at a hotel tonight. Kevin won't want to stay here."

Jericho tore his gaze away from the bookcase-lined wall and focused on Wayne. "I'm not sure. Kevin hasn't said."

Wayne made a sound somewhere between a laugh and a grunt. "You two could always sleep out here. As you can see, there's a bed and the heat works just fine. You'd have your own bathroom. It would save y'all some money. Not that Kevin's hurting for money, I guess."

"I'll suggest it." Jericho imagined Kevin probably wouldn't go for that, but he would ask. Silence dragged on between them as Jericho took in the small space. Light pink wallpaper covered the walls. White lace curtains covered the windows. It was over-the-top girlie, but he supposed that was the point. No matter how Jericho tried distracting himself, the busybody inside him kept rising to the surface. The sensation swelled until Jericho broke. "Do you mind if I ask you a personal question?"

For a moment, Wayne eyed him in silence. He looked so much like Kevin, except for his eyes. Those were gray and surrounded by laugh lines. They had the same serious demeanor, though. Finally, Wayne cleared his throat. "Since I get the feeling you're the only reason my son came to visit, ask away."

Jericho bit back a smile. He recognized a trap when he saw one. No way was he confirming that and reaffirming their beliefs that Kevin didn't want to be here. Instead, he chose to dig for info while he had the chance. "I get why Kevin hasn't visited in a few years, but why don't y'all come to see him? He obviously has plenty of room. In fact, knowing him, he would probably pay for your travel. I swear I'm not trying to be rude. I'm just curious."

Wayne didn't look the least bit offended. "Haven."

Against his will, Jericho's eyebrows rose. "What does he have to do with anything?"

With a sigh, Wayne sat on the edge of a very fragile-looking settee—like he half expected it to break beneath his weight. When it didn't, Wayne set his elbows on his knees and focused on Jericho. "I'm assuming you didn't know Kev before Haven."

Jericho shook his head.

Wayne gave him a sharp nod. "He was a different person. You never saw the boy without a huge smile on his face. He loved playing pranks on his mom and little sister. There was just this inner light shining from him. Then he got a football scholarship and moved to Texas. At first, we made tons of trips out that way. Hell, Minnie and I even talked about moving so we could be closer to Kevin. One day, out of the blue, he calls and announces he's gay." Wayne shook his head, as if he still couldn't believe it. "In a way, we weren't surprised. I mean, he'd never really tipped his hand or anything, but he also never dated. Minnie and I had a lot of discussions over the years about why he didn't show any interest in anyone. Obviously, we didn't care. We just want him to be happy, but then he tells us he's been dating someone. We were ecstatic. He'd been out of school for a while and he was working all the time. Minnie was certain he would die alone. Of course, we immediately made plans to visit to meet this mystery guy." A sad smile touched Wayne's lips. "We never expected the stranger we would be meeting would be our son. Kevin was unrecognizable. I mean, he looked the same, except he didn't. Even the way he held himself was different. You can't even imagine. He wouldn't even speak to us without looking at that boy for permission first. There was nothing healthy about their relationship." Jericho didn't like that picture. If anyone tried controlling Loyal like that... Jericho scared himself at the thought.

"They've been split up for a while," Jericho reminded him.

Wayne nodded. "True, but not visiting becomes a habit, and he still sounded the same every time we called—like Haven might be back any second. We'd just lost Brie not long before their split, and—honestly—we didn't have the strength to lose Kevin all over again when Haven shut us out of his life again."

Jericho's brow furrowed. "Did Haven forbid you from visiting?"

The way Wayne's mouth lifted in one corner held more bitterness than Jericho had seen in a while. "Oh, he was way too smart to come out and say the words, but we weren't welcome in their home. No one who stole a moment of Kevin's attention was welcomed to be in their lives. He's different with you, though. Maybe, since you have a son too, you see things differently than Haven. Truthfully, though, I think you're just a better person. Minnie and I are thankful Kevin met you."

Jericho's thoughts turned inward. He thanked every deity listening that Loyal had married Toby. Toby was a good man and would never shut Jericho out. Jericho hated that Kevin hadn't known a good man. He fought the urge to rub his chest. Jericho wanted to see the smiling prank-pulling boy Wayne described. The serious version of Kevin that Jericho knew was damn sexy, but he wanted all Kevin's facets. Jericho would make him happy.

As if thinking about Kevin conjured him, he appeared in the doorway. "Whoa, Mom. This is... a lot of pink."

Jericho chuckled at the horror in Kevin's voice. "I think that's the point. The place scares away the men."

Kevin's laughing gaze slid his way. For a moment, they held each other's stare. Jericho lost his breath.

"Exactly," Minnie said, pushing Kevin inside. "I want to read and nap in peace. With your dad retired, the television blares all hours of the day until I think I'll go insane. I need my own space."

"Your dad suggested we stay out here tonight, if you can handle the lace."

Kevin's gaze scoured the room. He looked thoughtful. "Sounds good to me, if it's all right with you."

Jericho shrugged. "Whatever you decide is good with me. After years of sleeping at the station, I can sleep anywhere. It takes a lot more than pink wallpaper to scare me."

Minnie and Wayne beamed over his willingness to stay. Wayne pushed to his feet. "I guess we should probably let y'all settle in. No doubt you're exhausted."

In truth, Jericho had a ton of pent-up energy, but the way Kevin watched him let Jericho know he would need it.

"Thank you for everything," Jericho said, crossing the room to Kevin's side.

Kevin slipped his arm around Jericho's waist. "I guess we'll see you in the morning. We'll probably go to bed soon." He sounded so casual, but Jericho could feel the change in Kevin's hold.

"Goodnight, boys. Love you, son," Minnie said, heading out. Wayne followed on her heels, pulling the door closed behind them.

Kevin kept his gaze locked on the door a minute longer before he focused on Jericho. The heat in his stare nearly blasted Jericho off his feet. "I'll get our bags from the car. You strip."

Jericho didn't need to be told twice. Kevin stole a quick kiss before leaving Jericho standing there dazed. He shook his head, trying to make his brain work. Sometimes, Kevin's kisses made him dumb. He peeled off his shirt.

Kevin reappeared with their luggage in hand. "You aren't nude."

A chuckle escaped Jericho. "You were too fast for me."

"I was gone at least ten minutes. Dad was still outside and wanted to talk. He likes you, by the way."

Jericho blinked. There was no way Kevin's kiss had scattered his thoughts for that long. Damn. He had it bad. He couldn't say that. "Maybe I just wanted to see what would happen if I disobeyed."

A wicked-looking smile stretched Kevin's lips. "It sounds a little like you want to get turned over my knee."

It was terrifying how fast his body reacted to the threat. His dick jumped to attention. When he spoke, lust tinged his words. "Maybe I do."

While holding Jericho's stare, Kevin dropped the bags, toed off his shoes, and peeled off his shirt. Jericho couldn't look away. Each second that passed brought him closer to coming in his jeans. His knees weakened as Kevin crossed the room. Kevin looked determined and turned on. It was a sexy combination.

"You made the choice. Remember that."

Dear god. Jericho could barely breathe. Kevin snagged his waist and hauled him toward the bed. In a flash, Jericho found his jeans around his ankles. A chuckle rose in his throat. He had never been depantsed so quickly. The room spun as Kevin hauled him forward and Jericho lost his balance with his ankles trapped. Then he was ass up, with his face pressed into the mattress, and across Kevin's lap before he knew how he got there. He tried drawing a breath. Kevin's palm collided with his bare ass. A moan escaped him with no input from his brain. His cock leaked onto Kevin's thighs.

"Is this what you wanted?" Kevin didn't give Jericho time to answer before another smack landed. It was loud but didn't hurt. Jericho was too turned on to feel pain. Kevin caressed the spot where his blow landed. His hand disappeared. Jericho started to push his way off Kevin's lap, but then another slap fell. "Be still." Jericho fell still. "That's it." Kevin swiped his hand down Jericho's crack, parting his cheeks. "I'm not done. Look at this delicious asshole." Jericho pressed his face harder against the mattress. He never expected to be embarrassed by the inspection, but he couldn't control the horror rising in him. Kevin rubbed his asshole. "I wonder what you do in the dark. Do you have toys? How far have you gone with experimenting?" Jericho scratched at the covers. Kevin pushed past the ring of tight muscles and fingered Jericho's ass. "How dirty do you get when you're alone, Jericho? Do you do this to yourself? Maybe you've even thought about something bigger. A dildo... a cucumber."

God help him. A moan vibrated from his chest, sounding like it came from his soul. His dick pumped out pre-cum at an alarming rate.

An evil-sounding chuckle caressed his ears. "You have thought about it. I could hear it in that moan, but have you done it?" A second finger joined the first inside Jericho. He pumped, mimicking sex. "Do you hide under the covers, muffling your cries while fucking yourself with whatever you can find? Is that the real reason you've stayed single in the last few years?" Terror raced through Jericho. He was trapped by desire and Kevin was dragging out his secrets. "Yeah, sexy. I'm not dumb. Loyal has been an adult for years, yet you've still not dated. You're so scared of yourself. I can feel it. I know you. In fact, I used to be you." Kevin pushed deeper and changed angles, hitting that internal button that nearly stole Jericho's orgasm. "I used to be terrified of my thoughts when I was turned on. I knew I wanted things I shouldn't. No one ever told me it was okay to want this." His fingers slipped from Jericho's asshole and another slap landed on his ass cheek. "People only talked about sex in whispers when I was a kid." He went back to fucking Jericho with his fingers. Jericho practically humped his lap, begging for more. "It's okay to be sexual," Kevin said, soothing Jericho. "There's nothing wrong about wanting this." He punctuated his words with massaging that spot that made Jericho wild. Pressure climbed his dick. He bit the covers to keep from begging. "Maybe one of these days it'll be my dick filling you. Would you let me, Jericho? Can I fuck you?"

A whimper filled the air. It took Jericho a second to realize the sound came from him.

"Don't come yet, sexy. If you come now, I'm putting my dick in your mouth. I'm not sure you want that. In fact, I'm positive you've never had a cock hitting the back of your throat."

Jericho couldn't help himself. He couldn't stop humping Kevin's thighs. Kevin was massaging just the right place and painting pictures in his mind. He needed release. His mind was ready to snap. In that moment, he was ready to suck all the dick. Anything for relief.

"Damn, Jericho. Your asshole is so tight. You

should see the way it sucks my fingers. So greedy to get fucked."

Jericho blew. There was no stopping the cum from jetting out, stealing his breath while Kevin stole his soul. He shamelessly rode the waves, fucking Kevin's fingers without a qualm. Jericho had never felt this way before. He never wanted it to stop. Being with Kevin was everything.

———

WATCHING JERICHO COME UNGLUED SNAPPED something inside Kevin. He scrambled to unzip his pants. The instant his erection spilled out; he was leading Jericho's mouth to it. He didn't see straight again until Jericho bobbed on his dick, bringing a bit of sanity back to him. Kevin stared down at Jericho sucking him. Jericho's cum coated his jeans. There was no shame between them. It was fucking beautiful. Tears stung Kevin's eyes as he realized the truth. He had never had this before. Maybe Haven had taught him to be open with his desires, but he had never set Kevin free. Jericho did. He let Kevin be real. More than that, he urged him to be better.

Kevin's fingers found Jericho's hair. He massaged the man's scalp as Jericho put his heart into his first blow job. Kevin knew then he would take Jericho's inexperienced enthusiasm over a professional seducer any day. Jericho was real in everything he did. He was amazing. Kevin wanted to keep him. Kevin would do whatever it took to make Jericho his and his alone. In fact, Kevin terrified himself in that moment, because he knew the truth. He wouldn't stop until Jericho was too addicted to him to leave. Jericho was his. Kevin wouldn't let anyone else have him.

SEVEN

KEVIN: *Thank you again for going with me to visit my parents. They loved you.*

Jericho: *Anytime. They're awesome. I loved the bed in your mom's she-shed. Five stars. Would recommend.*

Kevin: *Maybe I should build a little bungalow by the pool. What do you think? Would you hide from the world with me if I built us a place?*

Jericho: *Honestly? I can't think of anything I wouldn't do with you. You're pretty irresistible.*

Kevin: *Do you have a date tonight?*

Jericho: *Yeah. Sad panda.*

Kevin: *Tomorrow night, then?*

Jericho: *Definitely.*

LOYAL: *I HAVE A QUESTION.*

Jericho: *Okay.*

Loyal: *Well, it's more like a two-part inquiry.*

Jericho: *Okay.*

Loyal: *Are you dating Kevin—like for real? Not just as a client. AND do I have to call him Dad?*

Jericho: *You're so funny. I don't know how I had such a hilarious kid. We have been going on dates, for real. He's never been my client, so this has nothing to do with Cubs for Rent. You'd better never call anyone else Dad, and I don't know what we are yet. We're just seeing each other.*

Loyal: *Sometimes, I call Toby Daddy.*

Jericho: *I will fight you. Don't tell me things like that.*

Loyal: *LMAO! I like Kevin.*

Jericho: *Me too.*

MINNIE: *WE RESERVED THE CABIN FOR THE twenty-second and twenty-third. Kevin says he's in.*

Jericho: *I'm scheduled to work on the twenty-third, but someone offered to swap shifts, so I'm there.*

———

Kevin: *I know it's short notice, but I have to head to California to meet a client. Are you up for a quick overnight trip?*

Jericho: *I can't. I'm sorry.*

Kevin: *It's okay.*

Jericho: *Now I feel guilty. There's nothing I would rather do, but I have to be at work early tomorrow.*

Kevin: *Don't apologize. I understand.*

Jericho: *When you get back, you can tie me to the bed and punish me for not going.*

Kevin: *Deal.*

———

Loyal: *I thought you might have seen the story on the news about the huge warehouse fire and worry. Yes, Dad is there, but he's okay.*

Kevin: *Thank you for letting me know. I wanted to text him but figured he wouldn't have his phone if he was there.*

Loyal: *He's done this my whole life. Trust me, I have ways of checking on him. He's good.*

Kevin: *I really appreciate you keeping me posted.*

Loyal: *Anytime.*

EXHAUSTION WEIGHED HEAVILY ON JERICHO'S every muscle. A twenty-four-hour shift wasn't as easy as it used to be, especially when at least six hours of it was spent battling a huge warehouse fire. Some days, Jericho regretted putting his name on the Cubs for Rent site, selling his time. Other days, he recognized there was no place else he could make a thousand dollars for a few short hours of his time. That extra money was the only way Jericho could spoil Kevin the way he wanted. That made it worthwhile. As much as Jericho wanted to shower and fall into bed for days, he had been booked for the night. He had exactly four hours to shower, eat, and sleep. It wasn't near enough time. Jericho was so tired, breathing felt like a struggle. Maybe just a few seconds of closing his eyes before his shower would be okay. Jericho stripped and fell across the bed. A sigh fell from his lips as the world slipped into darkness.

Warm lips skimmed the small of Jericho's back. A moan rose in his throat. He peeked one eye open. A familiar scent washed over him. Expensive cologne that immediately had him going hard tickled his nose. The room was pitch dark. Panic slammed into Jericho. He shot upward. His gaze ate up the room. Red numbers on the face of his bedside clock proclaimed it was eleven.

"Goddamn it." Jericho was supposed to meet his date at seven. He had overslept. The light spilling from the bathroom outlined Kevin. Jericho scrambled from the bed. Guilt already ate him alive. "I'm so sorry, sweetie. I overslept. Someone hired me for the night and I fucking overslept."

Kevin made a calming gesture. "It's okay. You're fine. I knew you'd be too tired to go, so I called Toby earlier and asked him to make a counteroffer to your date on my behalf. I would pay him twice what he paid for him to switch to another night. My offer was accepted, and I left you to sleep."

Goddamn. Kevin was amazing, but Jericho couldn't have Kevin throwing his money around like that on his behalf. That made things weird, considering they slept together. "I'll pay you back." He scrubbed his hands over his face. Now that the initial panic passed, Jericho realized he didn't feel better. In fact, a few hours of sleep only made him crave more.

Kevin shook his head as he straightened the

bedcovers. He turned them back. "Get in. You're not ready to be up yet."

More grateful than he could communicate, Jericho climbed beneath the covers. Kevin draped them over him, tucking him in. Jericho wanted to thank him and tell him how appreciated he was, but Jericho's eyes were too heavy. One day soon, though, Jericho would have to make this up to Kevin. The man was way too good to him. He should tell him all the words.

Panic slammed into Jericho as he felt Kevin move away. Without any input from his brain, Jericho sat up like propelled by a grenade. "Kevin." He yelled like the man was three rooms over instead of three feet away. Jericho scrubbed a hand over his face. "Sorry. I think I was more asleep than awake just then."

"It's okay," Kevin soothed—like trying to ease him back to sleep as he moved to tuck Jericho in again.

Jericho snagged his waist and used what little energy he still had left to haul Kevin into bed with him. "You sleep with me," he grumbled as he snuggled the man tight like a teddy bear. He tossed a leg and arm across Kevin and used the man's chest as a pillow. Damn. Kevin was warm and comfy. Sleep was already luring him deeper.

"Jericho?"

"Mmmm?" Jericho hummed, barely conscious.

"I wish you were mine." Kevin said the words so quietly, Jericho wasn't sure he heard him right. He wanted to confess he already belonged to Kevin, but the exhaustion won. Jericho would make him see soon. He couldn't believe Kevin didn't already know.

KEVIN COULDN'T STOP WATCHING JERICHO SLEEP. He smelled like smoke and Kevin gave no fucks. Even in his sleep, Jericho looked exhausted. Kevin wondered if he ever got a real break. Between working twenty-four-hour shifts, accepting dates for Cubs for Rent, and trying to help Loyal walk again, Jericho didn't have much spare time. What little he got, Jericho spent with Kevin. They felt like a real couple. Kevin wanted to take care of him. The desire was twice as thick because Jericho didn't let him. He knew the only reason Jericho accepted Kevin paying off his date tonight was because he was too tired to fight. In the morning, he might have a few choice words to say about Kevin's high handedness, if he even remembered their talk. Until then, Kevin fully intended to enjoy every spare second with Jericho. Damn. He was sexy.

Jericho shifted. His leg moved higher, pinning Kevin to the bed with more force, while his hand moved lower, and slipped inside Kevin's shorts. Kevin drew a steady breath through his nose. Jericho was still asleep. He wasn't in charge of his actions. There would be no relief if he let his body react to Jericho's touch.

"Kevin."

The barely whispered sound of his name against his neck had Kevin going hard despite all his good intentions. He tried harder to breathe through the lust. He couldn't describe how it felt to know Jericho dreamed of him.

Jericho's fingers encircled Kevin's erection, proving he was somewhat awake. "I'm too tired to do anything else, but I want to touch you, okay?"

Even though Jericho sounded more asleep than anything, Kevin nodded. "Okay." He wasn't sure this wouldn't end up with him jerking off in Jericho's bathroom, but he couldn't turn down Jericho's attentions. Kevin squeezed his eyes closed as Jericho lightly stroked his cock. This was hell. This was heaven. Kevin wanted everything. He equally wanted to beg Jericho to stop teasing. His entire body burned. Every breath Jericho took brushed his throat. Kevin relished every sensation. He was completely lost to Jericho's touch.

Jericho's thumb scraped the slit of Kevin's crown before dragging pre-cum down Kevin's length. Kevin scratched at the covers. He had been turned on a lot since meeting Jericho. This was different. He was at Jericho's mercy. With his hand shoved inside Kevin's shorts and underwear, Jericho didn't have much range of motion. Not that it mattered. His touch was lazy, unhurried, and half asleep. The light brushing of fingers on his cock had Kevin writhing. He tasted blood from biting his lip. Despite the soft stroking, Kevin's balls were already drawn up tight. He was poised on the edge, ready to blow. Kevin fought the urge to shove Jericho's hand away so he could tug himself into orgasm. Instead, he stayed still, letting the torture continue. Kevin held his breath. Every muscle in his body strained. His heartbeat pounded in his ears as pressure beat at his crown. Starting at his balls, Jericho brushed his fingertips up Kevin's shaft. It was like he magically dragged Kevin's cum up his erection, because it burst from Kevin in a wave of blinding ecstasy. He moaned and gasped as pleasure rocked him. With Jericho's hand trapped inside his underwear, Kevin rocked upward against Jericho's palm, openly fucking the man's rough skin.

A soft snore caressed Kevin's ear. A chuckle stuck in Kevin's throat as his body shook. It looked like he would be sleeping in cum-covered clothes tonight, because he couldn't budge. Jericho's body draped over his like a two-ton weight Kevin couldn't lift. It wasn't that Jericho was too heavy for Kevin. Kevin's feelings weighed too much to give up Jericho's touch. It was love pinning him in place and Kevin didn't want to budge from beneath that load. After all, he had never expected to feel this way again. Jericho was just too much to resist for someone like Kevin. Someone broken.

EIGHT

JERICHO MADE it through most of another date night by picturing the way Kevin looked while kissing a path down his body. It was the only way he could keep his smile genuine. He wasn't loving this dating for money thing. It had been worth it though to see Kevin's face when he had opened that watch on Christmas, and how moved he looked each time Jericho paid at dinner. He knew Kevin wasn't used to being spoiled. Jericho wasn't like anyone else Kevin ever dated and Jericho needed Kevin to know it.

"Who is this?" The loud question sounded exactly like he was about to be undressed by someone's stare.

Jericho forced himself to focus on his

surroundings at the sudden appearance of some guy who looked to be close to twenty. He was blond and sparkly. Jericho felt old as fuck just looking at him, even though Blondy was looking at Jericho like he could be his next meal.

Dex Wise, the man who had hired him for the night, was tall, chiseled, and handsome. He was—according to Toby—the billionaire playboy of everyone's dreams. He did nothing for Jericho, but the blond sprite looked interested in all takers—like Dex and Jericho were the two-fer of his dreams.

Dex motioned Jericho's way. "Jericho meet Wren. Wren, Jericho." Dex sounded bored as hell. Yay! Go, him. He was so damn good at this escort thing. Jericho was wowing dates right and left.

Jericho worked up a genuine smile, despite the hopelessness of the situation, and shook Wren's hand. "Nice to meet you."

Wren's gaze moved down Jericho's body. "Why do you look familiar to me?"

"I have no idea." Jericho doubted they ran in the same circles. A pitch event for next season's fall lineup of TV shows wasn't the kind of thing Jericho warranted an invitation to under normal circumstances.

"Expensive suit. Bulgari necklace. Someone is

keeping you in style." Wren's smile brightened, making his light green eyes sparkle as they slid Dex's way. "Is it you, sweetie? You're not really known for passing out forty-grand necklaces to anyone. People usually fall at your feet for free."

Forty grand? Jericho thought he might hyperventilate.

Dex eyed the room, as if he couldn't wait to get away from this boring conversation. He didn't even look Wren's way as he responded. "Jericho's son is married to one of the Kodiaks."

"Oh," Wren said, his entire demeanor changed, turning serious. "Which one?"

"Toby," Jericho answered absently, still working his way past Kevin giving him a necklace that cost more than his truck.

Wren snapped his fingers. "That's why you look familiar to me. Damn. Your son looks just like you. It's uncanny. I mean, you've got a different build and the eyes are a bit different, but otherwise, you could be twins."

Jericho fought a snort. Everyone has a special talent. Wren's seemed to be blatant flattery.

Thankfully, Dex decided he was done. "It's been nice chatting with you, Wren. We have dinner reservations we can't miss."

Obviously good natured and too confident to take a personal hit at the dismissal, Wren winked. "No worries. If you two get bored afterward, Dex has my number. I know all the best ways to have fun." There was no mistaking the sexual innuendo in Wren's sultry tone as he took the opportunity to eye fuck Jericho one more time.

Dex's mouth lifted in one corner in a knowing smirk. Jericho's curiosity soared, but he kept his back teeth locked. Realization hit. He had been doing this dating for money thing for a little bit now, and he hadn't met a soul who made him chatter nonstop and ask millions of questions the way Kevin did. Like now, he was dying to know if Dex and Wren were sleeping together, but he wouldn't ask. He recognized it wasn't his business. Jericho didn't give any fucks if Kevin's life wasn't his business, he peppered the man like an interrogation each time he wondered about anything. Except for one topic, that is. He had yet to find the courage to ask Kevin if they were exclusive. Jericho was scared shitless they weren't. He wasn't ready to issue any ultimatums. For now, he just wanted to cling to Kevin any way he could.

JERICHO: *DID YOU GIVE ME A FORTY-THOUSAND-dollar necklace? Please tell me you didn't.*

Kevin: *No hablo inglés.*

Jericho: *Dear god. I've been wearing this thing everywhere. What if I lost it? I would die.*

Kevin: *You're adorable. Who told on me?*

Jericho: *Some guy at the thing I got paid to go to tonight.*

Kevin: ***sigh** I should've known someone would recognize the style. It was a gift, angel. It's rude to complain about a gift. Are you home now?*

Jericho: *Noted and yes. I just walked through the door.*

Kevin: *May I come to you?*

Jericho: *You know where to find the key. I need a shower.*

Kevin: *I'm about to get you even dirtier.*

Jericho: *I'm counting on it.*

KEVIN BRUSHED HIS PALM DOWN JERICHO'S chiseled torso, enjoying the way each bump felt beneath his hand. He fought a smile. It was obvious Jericho was flexing his muscles, like silently preening. The fact that he cared what Kevin thought of his body made Jericho twice as adorable.

"When do you find time to work out? You're always busy."

"There are a few weight machines at the station. It can get kind of boring around there."

It was the first words they had said to each other since Kevin walked through the door and into Jericho's arms. Some days, it felt like it had been weeks since he touched Jericho, rather than hours. They had been silently enjoying each other, as if Jericho felt the same.

While half perched on the counter in Jericho's kitchen, Jericho made no attempt to end their embrace. Jericho's countertops were lower than most, having been renovated to accommodate Loyal being in a wheelchair. Kevin was already picturing all the ways he could use their short height to his advantage.

"I've missed you a lot today."

Jericho's confession swelled Kevin's throat. Damn. He got it. "Same. I worried you might meet some celebrity tonight and I would never see you again."

A sexy-sounding rumble of laughter vibrated from Jericho's chest. "I'm pretty sure everyone there was too busy trying to catch sight of their own reflections to see anyone else."

Kevin snorted at the picture Jericho painted. He believed it. Before he could say as much, Jericho blew him away.

"Not that you have anything to worry about. I'm beyond satisfied with you. You're the only person to catch my attention in years. I'm not looking elsewhere and letting you get away."

Kevin was stupid in love with Jericho. He didn't know where to go with it. All he knew was, Jericho was in his arms right now. He had to make sure Jericho stayed satisfied.

Kevin lifted Jericho onto the counter.

A loud laugh escaped Jericho as he clung to Kevin's shoulders. "You know most people can't manhandle me like this."

"Are you complaining?" Kevin asked, nuzzling Jericho's neck.

Jericho's voice turned breathless. "Not at all." He obediently lifted his arms, letting Kevin have his shirt.

Kevin tossed it aside and went back to nibbling Jericho's skin. He went to work on Jericho's pants. Kevin didn't have to work hard. Jericho had already changed into his pajamas before Kevin arrived. With the slightest tug, he had Jericho's erection in his hand. "I dozed off after work," Kevin said, moving to lick Jericho's nipple. "And dreamed about you," he added, sliding lower. "I was sucking your dick." Kevin bent and licked Jericho's crown. His eyes fell closed at Jericho's first moan. Jericho's pleasure always got Kevin high. He stroked Jericho's length. "Then all these people appeared, watching us. But you wouldn't let me stop. You became quite the shameless exhibitionist with your cock in my mouth. I woke up hard and leaking in my underwear."

"Fuck," Jericho breathed, snagging Kevin's hair and tugging, leading him toward where he wanted him. "Please tell me you couldn't stop yourself from jacking off to the fantasy of me."

"You know it." It was the last chance Kevin got to speak. Jericho fucked his mouth without mercy. He held Kevin's hair and pumped into his throat. His moans reverberated from the walls. He was open in his need for Kevin. There was nothing fake about Jericho and it was beautiful. Kevin would give him the world. All he wanted was Jericho's happiness.

With a shout, hot cum filled Kevin's mouth. He tried swallowing as fast as he could. Jericho tugged, urging Kevin back to his mouth. He kissed Kevin deep, uncaring of the cum and saliva coating his chin. Jericho was wild in his arms, tearing at Kevin's clothes and skin, trying to get closer. For the first time in more years than he could count, Kevin felt it —triumph. He could make Jericho love him. This wasn't a passing affair. They weren't killing time together. This was real. Jericho was his. He would love Kevin and they would always be happy. Kevin would have a good life with Jericho. He felt it in his bones.

NINE

IN THE THREE months Jericho had been seeing Kevin, he had done a damn good job of avoiding Haven. He should have known it was only a matter of time before they crossed paths. Between Haven befriending Jericho's family and them working for Cubs for Rent, running into each other was inevitable. With directions to a job in Terrell Hills in hand, Jericho headed to his truck. When he spotted Haven heading for Toby and Loyal's back door, he put his head down and barreled ahead, refusing to acknowledge him. Jericho almost made it to his truck.

"Jericho, hold up."

Jericho pasted on a fake smile and turned. "Hey." He folded the paper Loyal had printed for him to give his hands something to do. Haven looked uncomfortable and worried. Jericho tried hardening his heart against it. They would never be friends. "Did you need something, Mister? Or is it Haven? Honestly, I'm not sure what to call you anymore."

"Either is fine. I go by both." He looked more uncomfortable by the second. "I mean, my name is Haven, but I've gone by Mister for a long time and that's also my author name, so that's what almost everyone calls me, except for Kevin, but whatever. I'll answer to either." Haven took a breath, visibly trying to stop the rambling. "Anyhow, I'll try to keep this short, since it's obvious you don't want to talk to me. I'm sorry. I've tried texting to apologize sooner, but you either haven't gotten my messages or you're ignoring me. Anyhow, Loyal is your son and he didn't deserve my outburst. When it comes to Kevin, I've never had good sense, but I get that I was wrong. Obviously, your loyalty will always be with your family, but I've apologized to everyone else, including Kevin. You deserve to be included." Haven shifted from one foot to the other. It was getting harder to be angry, and then Haven took the wind from Jericho's bitter sails. "It's just that I thought we were on our way to becoming friends and then I fucked things up. While I'm used to always being a screw up, I'm not used to having friends. Even though I'm not very good at it, I'd really hoped we could try again. I think you're awesome. I'm sorry that I'm not."

"I'm dating Kevin." God help him. Jericho had no idea why he said it. The words just burst from his chest with no input from his brain. The worst part was he hadn't truly established that Kevin and he were in an actual relationship, so he might have totally screwed up everything.

Haven's expression snapped closed. He visibly fought to keep his thoughts private. "I see."

Did he? Because Jericho wasn't sure even he did, and he was the one who had blurted out that bullshit with zero input from Kevin. Goddamn. He didn't know what to do. Discomfort took control of Jericho's tongue and ran. "I just thought you should know. You're right. I thought we would be friends too. We have a lot in common, but then you lashed out at Toby and tried hurting my son the second you saw Toby with Kevin. I get that wasn't really your intentions and you were just upset, but you could've done some real damage to someone already in a fragile state." Jericho took a breath, hoping to stop the deluge of words. It didn't work. "I mean, everything worked out, but when you stormed off and the boys headed to Vegas to get married, Kevin and I went too. We clicked. It's just that—"

"Stop," Haven said, holding up his hand and cutting Jericho's diarrhea of the mouth short. Haven's chest expanded as he took a deep breath. His gaze never wavered from Jericho—like pain had him incapable of looking away from the thing that attacked his heart. "Kevin is free to date whoever he wants." Funny how it sounded like a lie, but Haven kept talking. "Obviously, you're also free to do whatever you want. Neither of you owe me anything." He cleared his throat. It sounded painful. "Kevin is amazing." Haven visibly swallowed. "He deserves to be happy. I hope you don't... fuck it. I can't do this." Haven walked away without looking back. Jericho stared after him with his heart in his throat. There was a real possibility Jericho had just ruined any chance he had of having a real relationship with Kevin. He didn't know where to go with that. All Jericho knew was he had to fix this. He had to talk to Kevin and make things real. There was no other option to Jericho's heart.

———

FOR THE PAST FOUR HOURS, SINCE LEAVING

Jericho alone in bed, Kevin had fought the urge to go home. He had a ton of paperwork and no drive. Jericho's nude body beneath his covers called to Kevin on a visceral level. He knew Jericho wasn't still lounging in his bed, but still. Kevin was on edge. He wanted to be with Jericho. Unfortunately, Jericho had a job tonight, working for Cubs for Rent. While Kevin wasn't in love with that, he also was in no position to argue. No matter how often he told himself that they needed to talk about their future, his lips never moved. He needed to know where he stood. Kevin was scared shitless he wasn't standing where he thought he was in Jericho's life. It was better to have some of Jericho than none, but Kevin wanted all of him.

"Mr. Abbot, you have a visitor."

Kevin glanced up from the paperwork on his desk. Penny, his receptionist, stood in the doorway, waiting for him to acknowledge her words. Kevin didn't think he had any appointments today. Of course, his mind had been so full of Jericho, he wasn't sure. He flashed the tiny red-haired woman who had worked for him since he moved to Austin a small smile. "Thanks, Penny."

He really didn't think he was expecting anyone. Maybe it was Jericho. Once that thought hit, there was no going back. Kevin pushed to his feet and headed for the front. An out-of-control smile pulled at his lips. He missed Jericho, which was crazy. It had only been a few hours since he had last seen the man. In a flash, Kevin's feet froze to the floor. His smile fell. Haven stood, hands behind his back and waiting. Kevin's mind blanked as his feelings went into hiding—the way they always did to save themselves from Haven's destruction.

"What are you doing here?" From the corner of his eye, Kevin saw Penny's head snap up, obviously put on alert by Kevin's tone.

Haven looked a wreck—like he was still sickening perfection, but his eyes looked crazed. He was a mess on the inside. Kevin would know that look anywhere. Haven scrubbed the back of his neck. "Is there any way we can talk for a minute? Outside?"

Something felt... wrong. "All right." Kevin glanced Penny's way. "If anyone calls, just take a message. I'll be back in a minute."

Penny flashed him a worried-looking smile. Kevin buried his trepidation and followed Haven out the door. Once they were out of earshot, Kevin crossed his arms over his chest and dove in. "What do you need, Haven?"

Haven crossed his arms, matching Kevin's pose before quickly dropping his arms again. Finally, his gaze locked on to Kevin. Kevin almost took a step back. "How can you do it?"

Kevin's eyebrows tried climbing to his hairline. "Do what?"

"Move on from this," Haven said, motioning between them. "How could you let us go and start dating Jericho?"

With a deep breath, Kevin dropped his confrontational stance and moved to sit on a nearby stone bench. The spot was where smokers took their breaks and smelled like stale cigarettes, but it was in the shade. Kevin swallowed past the lump in his throat. "How did you find out about Jericho?"

"He told me." There was no triumph or anger in those words, merely the same hurt Haven had shown since turning up. Haven blinked and looked up for a second as if fighting tears. He took a breath before meeting Kevin's stare again. "I know I messed up, but a part of me has always thought it would be us to the very end. Like it was always supposed to be us."

Kevin tried hard to breathe. He couldn't let Haven push him into having heart issues today, but neither could he back down. His watch started beeping—like a fuck you to Kevin's good intentions.

Kevin embraced his anger with both arms, since it was too late. "You're the one who decided we weren't enough for you."

Haven scrubbed his hands through his hair and paced away before moving back to hover over Kevin. "I've made a lot of mistakes, Kev, but you know I never touched Sawyer. It was never sexual with him."

Goddamn. Would this ever stop? Sometimes, Kevin wondered if he was cursed. Every time he found a little bit of happiness, he paid for it. His chest hurt. "I don't know a damn thing. All I have is your word. Not that it matters if you never touched him; you gave him all your time. Every time I turned around, you were with him. He had your heart." Kevin came to his feet. His temper rose by the second. He never wanted to hear Sawyer's name again for as long as he lived. Kevin had come in second to that guy for way too long. That guy had already stolen everything. "You can say anything you want, Haven, but you know damn well he was under your skin. You wanted him, whether you acted on it or not. I was supposed to be your life. I was the one always on my knees. He owned your heart and every thought in your head while I literally begged for a single ounce of your attention." Haven took a step back in the face of Kevin's fury, but it was too late. Something inside Kevin snapped. He was done playing. All the times he had stayed silent, been the good boy, rose to the surface and blasted out at Haven now. "Every night, you were with him while I fucking pleaded for you to notice me. You were the greatest love of my life and I meant nothing while he meant everything. I am your goddamn husband. You were the one for me."

"Oh."

Kevin's head snapped around at the quietly spoken word. Jericho stood nearby, holding a bouquet of roses. Everything was so dark inside Kevin's mind. He was so goddamn angry. It took him a second for him to realize what he had said and why Jericho looked so crushed.

Jericho's gaze moved between them. His expression closed, shutting Kevin out. "I just came by to take you to lunch, but I see you're busy... with your husband, apparently."

"No," Kevin said, trying to rush to explain.

Jericho wasn't having it. "It's okay. I get it. I..." Jericho's shoulders fell and he walked away without bothering to finish.

Kevin watched him go with his heart in his throat. His gaze slid Haven's way. He had never hated anyone more. It sat on his chest and throat, crushing the life from Kevin. His eyes burned. He didn't know how one person could steal so much from someone they pledged to love until death.

Haven stared back at Kevin, looking shocked—like he hadn't intended to destroy Kevin's life all over again. Something inside Kevin shriveled and died. When he spoke, Kevin's voice sounded as raw as he felt. "In all my life, I never thought I would say this to anyone. I wish you were dead." He walked away, ashamed of himself and sick. His watch beeped nonstop, making his head hurt. Maybe his heart would finally give out. Kevin was tired. Just exhausted. He didn't know how to keep losing like this. All he knew was that living without Jericho wasn't an option. Kevin's heart wouldn't withstand the blow. There wasn't much left of him to shatter.

JERICHO DROVE ON AUTOPILOT WITH NO destination in mind. His phone rang several times, but he ignored it. He should have known Kevin was too good to be true. Things had been too easy. Jericho's life was never simple. He knew he should let himself think. Jericho was terrified to go down that path. He understood the overall truth. The big picture wasn't hard to miss. Jericho had fallen in love with someone else's husband. That was a stiff blow.

Realistically, Jericho understood the pair were split. There was too much rage in Kevin to believe otherwise. But there was also too much anger in Kevin for Jericho to believe they were over. It was one thing to be bitter. Hell, Jericho was still resentful as fuck with his ex-wife and they had been done for more than seventeen years. This was different. Kevin openly hurt. Open wounds meant fresh lashes from someone still capable of causing pain. Kevin wasn't over Haven. That meant he would likely go back to Haven one day—just as Kevin's parents feared. It was best Jericho walked away now before he ended up even more crushed. He would slip away from things. Kevin had never said they were officially dating, and Jericho knew why now. There was no need to talk about it. Kevin and Haven were just two people Jericho had recently met and he would stop now. He wouldn't talk to either man again. In fact, he would withdraw his name from Toby's website. That way, there was no chance he would run into either man at any event. He would get out of their way.

Jericho rubbed his chest. He stared at the outside

of his house with no desire to climb from his truck. Everything was empty. He had lived his life for his son, and now his son was married. Jericho was old and alone. Doing the right thing always cost him everything. He didn't regret staying single all these years. Loyal was more important to him than anything, but damn. He really was old and alone. Things looked bleak and... just empty now.

Jericho pushed open the driver's side door. His body felt heavy as he climbed from the truck. He had let Kevin in. Jericho had shown a side of himself he hadn't given anyone else. There was a small part of him, though, that had always known. A tiny sliver of his heart had seen this coming. The way Haven had behaved when he had seen Kevin with Toby, knowing full well Toby had only been hired to go out with Kevin; people didn't act crazy like that over just anyone. Kevin was amazing. Jericho had wanted to believe Haven was reacting to losing someone so unbelievable. He supposed Haven was only reacting to losing someone more important to him than his pride—his husband.

Jericho's knees nearly buckled at the thought. Somehow, he made it inside. He headed straight for the freezer. A bottle of Ciroc called his name. He didn't bother with a glass. Instead, Jericho headed out back. Sometimes, the quiet and his rocking chair were all he needed. He doubted the combo would do him much good today, but he also had liquor. With enough of all three, he might forget. At least for a little while.

His phone buzzed several times until Jericho turned off the device. There was nothing he was willing to hear from anyone right now. Even if it wasn't Kevin-related, Jericho wasn't in the right headspace to talk to anyone.

"Goddamn. You don't make it easy to find you, do you?" Haven didn't wait for Jericho's answer. "I had to call and beg Loyal to take mercy on me when you didn't answer the door. He said you like to sit back here, so I took a chance. Speaking of Loyal, he said he reassigned your date to someone else, since you didn't show."

Fuck. He had forgotten about his scheduled date. How long had he been driving around aimlessly? Jericho chugged his vodka to stop all the hateful words that crowded his tongue at Haven's appearance. It didn't work as well as he hoped. "What do you want?"

With no care to Jericho's thoughts on the matter, Haven claimed the chair beside him. "This is a nice place. Quiet. Pretty."

Jericho rolled his eyes. "Quaint. I get it. I'm poor." Fuck. To think he once liked Haven.

"That's not what I meant at all. Before Kevin, I didn't have anything. He's the one who worked while I wrote my books. Everything I am is because of him. I know what you think, but you're wrong. By the first of next week, we won't be married any longer. That's our final court date. My lawyer tells me the judge will sign all the paperwork and it'll be done. Just like that. Like I never existed."

Jericho couldn't even look at him. Logically, Jericho recognized it wasn't Haven's fault that Kevin hadn't told Jericho they were married. Not that it mattered all that much. Like Haven said, they were getting divorced. The problem was, Kevin wasn't over the guy. Jericho couldn't compete.

For a long time, they sat side by side in silence, staring at nothing while lost in their thoughts. Jericho passed the vodka Haven's way. Haven turned it up before passing it back. It didn't matter they had lost the same man. Jericho had never been one to celebrate anyone's misery.

After some time passed and between them the bottle got low, Jericho lost his unwillingness to speak. "What happened between you two anyhow? Like you really fucked him up. He has heart problems and shit because of you."

Haven slid deeper in his seat and set the rocking chair in motion. "I was young and dumb."

Jericho snorted. "You still are."

"True," Haven said without an ounce of irritation. "Kevin is ten years older than me. We met when I was eighteen and started hitting the clubs. I've always been controlling and possessive, but when I met Kevin, all that doubled. He was already making good money and had a nice house. Nothing like he does here in Austin, but he was on his way. Once he was mine, I dug my heels into his life, because I needed him way more than he needed me. By the time I turned twenty, I was already under his roof and determined to hang on to him in every way. He worked crazy hours, but he always put me first. Then, he landed his first multimillion-dollar sale. Things exploded. People loved him. He was supporting me so I could follow my dream of becoming an author. That meant I was always home. Like I said, I was young. I didn't see that support as Kevin showing me his love. Instead, I turned bitter. He was mine, but he was always gone, and I was always alone. When he was home, he was tired and didn't want to go anywhere with me."

Haven took another swig of the vodka. When he spoke again, Jericho could hear the burn of the alcohol in his throat. "One night, everything came to a head for me. We were getting ready to go out for the first time in forever. He got a call and had to go. It was always like that back then. He was trying so hard to make a name for himself, and all I saw was him running out on me again. I couldn't see that he was killing himself for us. It didn't feel like it. It felt like I was last in his life." A derisive-sounding snort escaped Haven. "I tried ordering him to stay with me. In the past, he never would've defied me. He just apologized and left. So I went out alone. I should've stayed home," Haven said as if more for himself.

After a second, he cleared his throat and got back on track. "I went to this BDSM club where I usually took Kevin. There was this boy there who looked to be the same age I was when I started going, but one glance at him said he didn't have an ounce of dominance in him. He was there looking for someone like me. Turned out, Sawyer was nineteen and had just escaped an abusive daddy. He was looking for protection from someone new. I kept him company. Warned him away from men I knew to be too rough. He hung on every word I said. Looked at me the way Kevin used to. I had forgotten what it was like to feel that way. Powerful. Hell, maybe it was just that seven-year itch people talk about. I was twenty-five and stuck in the house alone most of the time. It was nice to be noticed again. Nothing happened. I went home to Kevin. I always went home to Kevin," Haven said, sounding lost again.

"But I was done being ignored. Every chance I got, I met Sawyer. I thought, as long as I didn't sleep with him, it was fine. In fact, Kevin knew about him. I explained that he had been abused and didn't need to be at the club unescorted until he found a new protector. Kevin seemed okay with it, at first. But it didn't take long for him to see the truth: it was a full-blown emotional affair. Maybe I didn't touch him, but I wanted to, and Kevin isn't stupid. I got really good at lying to myself. I told myself we were just friends, completely convinced I could make it true as long as I stuck to my guns. Then, one night, Kevin blew up at me. He had never yelled before that night. I was furious at him for challenging me. All I saw was his defiance. I couldn't see that he was fighting *for* me. He wanted me to punish him and remember what that was like. Instead, I just wanted to find Sawyer and go back to being someone's sole focus. So I stormed out, stopped at the first fetish shop I passed, and bought Sawyer a collar." Haven's knee bobbed. He drank some more liquor and cleared his throat. Still, he kept his gaze on the setting sun.

"Back then, I knew just enough about being a master to be dangerous. I can still see Sawyer's light green eyes lighting up as I snapped that collar around his neck. In that moment, everything inside my head cleared, and I saw myself in a way I never had before. I was wrong. Kevin was sacrificing everything for me, and I was wrong. Before I could run away, back home to where I belonged, Sawyer shot forward and kissed me. Kevin was sitting in the corner watching the whole thing. He had followed me from the second I left. There wasn't a moment with Sawyer he missed. He watched me choose Sawyer." Haven rubbed his chest. "Goddamn. Some things you can't take back." Haven cleared his throat again. "Anyhow, I've spent the last two years swinging wildly between trying to win him back and setting him free. I refused to file for divorce, and he didn't either, so I thought I had hope. Until three months ago, that is. That's when I got hit with papers." He finally looked Jericho's way. "Right after he started dating you."

The truth hit Jericho. "You knew the moment we started dating, didn't you?"

Haven nodded and looked away. "I still keep an eye on him. He may be yours now, but—to me—he'll always be mine. It didn't really feel real until you said the words earlier. I thought—hoped—you were only friends."

Jericho snorted. "From the rage I saw today, he's still yours. Maybe I am just a friend."

"He told me he wishes I was dead. I don't think hate runs much deeper than that. He's over me. I broke something in him. Other than his heart, that is. He just..." Haven's hands rose and fell. "... hates me. I'll never be sorry enough or broken enough to soothe what I did. He's done." Haven looked his way. His stare was so intense, Jericho got the urge to run. "This is the only way I can fix this. You have to love him better than I did. He won't let me do it any longer. So, you have to. Kevin isn't made to be alone. His emotions run too deep. You're the one he chose, so don't let him down like I did. He needs you."

Jericho looked away from Haven's intensity. Sometimes, he caught flashes of the Dom inside Haven. He didn't have that. Maybe that was why Kevin couldn't love him. Silence dragged on. Jericho had to fill it. "What happened with Sawyer?"

Haven didn't answer for so long that Jericho had given up by the time he finally spoke. "Two days after I gave him that collar, he showed up at the club wearing it and looking for me. I wasn't there, but his ex was. He didn't survive."

Jericho's eyes fell closed.

"Just another black mark on my soul," Haven said, sounding empty. "Being the bad guy is so much harder than anyone ever tells you."

Damned if Jericho knew the right thing to do. Of course, that might have a little bit to do with the copious amount of liquor flowing through his veins. Too bad it didn't kill the pain. Haven might be the bad guy, but Kevin had called him *"the one."* It seemed good guys did always finish last. No big surprise there.

As Kevin's knuckles landed on Toby's door, Kevin questioned his sanity for coming here. Jericho's words about the Kodiak brothers inviting Kevin into their lives because he was wanted kept coming back to Kevin. He hoped that was true, because he didn't have anywhere else to go. Haven had isolated him from everyone years ago. At one time, Toby had felt like a friend. Kevin needed that now. He almost gave up hope of anyone answering, when the door finally swung wide. Loyal was on the other side. He looked more than a little surprised to find Kevin standing there.

"Hey."

Kevin waved. "Hi." To Kevin's horror, his voice broke and the word was barely a whisper.

"This explains a lot," Loyal said more for himself. He rolled his chair back a few feet. "Come in."

Kevin's feet refused to budge. "Maybe I shouldn't have come here." A tear rolled down his cheek and Kevin quickly wiped it away. He refused to break.

"I'm glad you're here. Orion and Tucker took the boat out and Toby had to go to Tanner's. I've been trying to get the coffee from the cabinet for more than fifteen minutes now, but I used all my strength at therapy earlier. I need someone tall to help me."

Maybe it was bullshit to soothe Kevin's pride, but Kevin had to take it. Otherwise, he might do anything. "Okay." Kevin stepped inside and closed the door. He prayed he wasn't making a huge mistake. This was Jericho's son. As soon as the thought floated through his mind, Kevin's shoulders squared. This was Jericho's son. He needed help. Kevin felt closer to Jericho being here, doing something for the love of his life's son. "Point the way." Kevin would reach the hell out of that coffee—like Jericho would want him to do.

Loyal led the way to the kitchen.

Kevin followed at a slower pace.

Loyal glanced over his shoulder as he cleared the kitchen door. "Second door from the fridge. Three shelves up."

With a nod, Kevin moved to the cabinet and easily snagged the coffee before moving toward the pot. "How strong do you like it? I'll fix it."

"Thank you. I really appreciate it. If it's strong enough to peel paint, it might keep me awake a few more hours until Toby gets home. I'm exhausted."

Kevin filled the filter with grounds. With his gaze locked on his task, he tried not to think about Jericho's expression as he learned Kevin was married. Loyal looked so much like his dad. It was hard.

"You love my dad, don't you?"

Kevin shot a nervous look over his shoulder at the question. It seemed wrong to admit such a thing to Loyal when he hadn't said the words to Jericho, but neither could he deny it. "Yes." Kevin went back to focusing on his task. "He's a good man. It's impossible not to love him. I don't deserve to be loved back, though. I pretty much suck at... everything, I suppose."

"Me too," Loyal surprised him by saying. "I think that's pretty much a requirement of earning my dad's love."

"You're his son. Loving you is literally the biggest requirement of his job. I have nothing to recommend me."

"He chose you." Loyal said the words so seriously that Kevin found himself focused on him and scared to blink. He needed hope. "All my life, I watched people chase my dad. He's my dad, but I'm not blind to his appeal. He's steady and good looking. Not to mention, he has a good job and is genuinely nice. He's practically beating people off with a stick, dodging phone numbers like a pro for literally years. Yet, he chose you." A small smile touched Loyal's lips and he looked more like Jericho in that moment than ever before. "He won't let Haven come between you. I promise if you show up for him, Dad will never stop showing up for you."

Kevin wasn't surprised Loyal knew this was about Haven. He had probably already talked to his dad. Kevin couldn't imagine Jericho not telling Loyal everything. "I'm scared of myself," Kevin said, admitting something he never had. "I'm scared that

Haven broke something in me, making me unlovable." Hell, even his parents didn't visit anymore. Maybe he was just an empty shell now. "I'm not who I used to be before him, and I never will be again."

A bright smile lit Loyal's entire face. He really was a gorgeous boy. It was no wonder Jericho was so proud of him. He was an amazing human. "I think you're exactly what Dad needs. You won't take him for granted. You've already seen what's it's like to love a shitty man. Now you'll do anything to hang on to a good one. If I could've picked anyone for him, it would be you. Don't give up. He's not the type to let anyone else steal what's his and he definitely thinks of you as his. I wish you could see the way he lights up when he talks about you. I think you're it for him." Before Kevin could think of a way to respond, an adorable spark of irritation crossed Loyal's features. "What is that beeping? It's driving me nuts."

Kevin pulled a face. "Sorry. It's my watch. Your dad bought it for me, and I don't know how to make it stop."

Loyal chuckled. "Leave it to Dad to buy something super annoying that never stops making noise so he's never far from your mind."

A smile tugged at the corners of Kevin's mouth. A ridiculous image came to mind of Jericho talking nonstop. It was just like him to buy something that never stopped making noise. Kevin would make this right. He had to. Living without Jericho's constant chatter wasn't an option. He loved the sound of Jericho's voice too much to let go.

TEN

KEVIN WAS MORE than halfway to Jericho's house, lost in thought, before he realized he was behind Jericho's truck. His heartbeat pounded in his ears. What if Jericho spotted him and decided to keep driving? Kevin couldn't blame him. Each time he played yesterday's scene over in his head, he looked worse. Kevin could still see Jericho standing there with flowers. He was so sexy and devastated by Kevin's secrets. Kevin had no excuse for not telling Jericho he was married. The man had simply sideswiped him. He hadn't planned to meet anyone and then Jericho was there, stealing his heart.

Truthfully, he had hoped to get quietly divorced and move along without acknowledging it. Now he recognized how shitty that was. Jericho deserved to know everything. Kevin felt like he had tricked Jericho into caring about him under false pretenses. He couldn't explain why he hadn't divorced Haven sooner. Maybe because he felt like a failure. His parents had tried telling him that marrying someone so much younger than him was a mistake. Then they had learned Kevin was supporting him financially while Haven wrote. The condescension had been thick. For Haven to prove them right and Kevin wrong, it stung.

None of that mattered now. Jericho was the one Kevin wanted, but he wasn't sure he could win him. He had to find a way. Kevin's watch started beeping again. He tried taking a calming breath. After a second, it stopped.

Kevin breathed a sigh of relief when Jericho pulled into his driveway. Jericho was already avoiding his calls and texts. This was the only avenue left for Kevin. While Kevin practically leapt from his car, Jericho took his time exiting his truck. He slowly slid from inside while balancing two grocery bags. It couldn't have been more obvious he dreaded a confrontation.

Kevin waited patiently. He would wait forever

for someone who treated him as wonderful as Jericho did. Kevin bit his bottom lip at the first full glimpse of Jericho. He was so gorgeous. Kevin couldn't lose him.

"Hi."

Jericho didn't look thrilled. "Hey."

Kevin motioned at nothing. "I tried to call before coming over, but you know..." Actually, he had tried calling all night, but that was beside the point.

"Yeah."

Damn. It wasn't going well. His watch started beeping again. Jericho's gaze dropped to Kevin's wrist. Kevin covered the watch with his other hand, hoping to smother the sound. He took a breath and dove in. "I'm sorry I didn't tell you I'm married."

"I don't care about that."

Confusion had Kevin's forehead furrowing. "Then why are you avoiding me?"

Jericho took an audible breath and shifted the grocery bags he held. "I came by yesterday, hoping to talk to you about making this thing real. I didn't want to question anymore if we were a couple or if we were just casually dating. You felt like mine. Then I got there in time to hear you tell Haven he's the one for you. I just..." Jericho blew out a breath and glanced away for a second before meeting his stare once more. "Look, I get it. You're not ready for me. You haven't had seventeen years to put the bitterness of disappointment behind you when the person you planned to spend the rest of your life with turned into a complete stranger you didn't recognize at all." Damn. Kevin had never had his relationship with Haven nailed so perfectly. He was speechless, which was just as well. Jericho wasn't finished. "The thing is, sweetie, it has been seventeen years since my divorce, and I am ready for you. I'm not getting any younger and I've already spent my best years on the bench. Granted, I did it more for Loyal than anything else. No matter the reason, those years are gone for me. I refuse to spend the next seventeen years waiting for you to figure out if I'm enough." Jericho shrugged, looking sad. "Haven is a lot of things I'll never be. He's young and has this whole lifestyle thing I don't get. Y'all have history and he already has your heart. I'm just some guy." Jericho blinked as if saying the words made him want to cry. "That's all I'll ever be. Maybe you were never meant to look my way." He glanced down at the groceries he held. Kevin swore he could feel the hurt rolling off him in waves. It nearly took out Kevin's knees. He wasn't used to being the bad guy. "I have to get these groceries in the house. It's one of the few things I'm good at. You know, keeping food at its proper temperature. Just what everyone's looking for in a man." Jericho walked away, leaving Kevin behind without another word.

A smile stretched Kevin's lips. His watch finally stopped beeping. "You're a huge weirdo, did you know that?" Jericho stopped midway to the house and looked Kevin's way at the claim. Kevin couldn't stop smiling. "You're really just painfully awkward sometimes and you say the oddest shit. Just whatever pops into your head. And I'm just..." Kevin's hands rose and fell, showing he had nothing. "... completely in love with you," he finished, lacking any other way of describing how Jericho had taken over his life. Unexpectedly, his throat swelled. "Haven isn't the one for me. I was wrong about him, and I'm scared shitless to be wrong about you too. But I absolutely love you and want to try. You're right. Maybe I'm not ready, but I have to do it anyhow, because I can't risk letting you slip away."

Jericho moved from one foot to the other. He looked like a man who didn't want to hope. "Would you like to come in?"

With a nod and optimism filling his chest, Kevin followed Jericho to the door. As Jericho jammed his keys in the lock, Kevin broke. He molded against Jericho's back and wrapped his arms around him. With his forehead pressed to Jericho's shoulder, Kevin held on, trying to ease his soul. He hadn't simply been saying the words. Kevin loved him. He couldn't lose him. The fucking watch started beeping again.

Jericho dropped his chin and kissed the arm Kevin had wrapped around his neck. "We're okay, baby. Just come inside."

Kevin took a step back, giving Jericho his space. His eyes burned. Jericho said they were okay, but Kevin didn't feel it. Nonetheless, he followed Jericho inside and hoped for the best. Jericho set his bags down inside the kitchen and started unpacking while Kevin waited with his heart in his throat. Jericho opened the fridge. After putting a few things in, he came out with the flowers from yesterday.

He held them out for Kevin. "I didn't have the heart to throw them away."

As Kevin reached for the bouquet of red roses, he swallowed past the lump in his throat. He eyed them. They were a little wilted, but he loved them. "No one has ever bought me flowers."

Jericho's eyebrows snapped together. "Seriously?

I figured you've been getting flowers every day, and I wasn't original."

Kevin felt a bit stupid for his inability to stop looking at the roses. Confessions kept coming. "I'm not sure I've ever mattered very much to anyone."

"You mean everything to me."

Kevin's gaze snapped to Jericho. He looked sincere. "I would never intentionally hurt you." Kevin's voice cracked. "I know I'm a bitter person with a lot of anger in my heart, but that didn't stop you from crawling under my skin. What you think about me matters—"

"I love you." Jericho said the words calmly—like they were real and serious. He didn't make Kevin beg or submit. Jericho didn't make Kevin less so he could be more. Kevin couldn't fight the burning behind his eyes. Jericho didn't stop there. "To me, you're amazing and irreplaceable. You don't have to be angry here."

"Why are you always so calm and steady?" Even though the question popped from Kevin with no input from his brain, he needed the answer. Jericho was so much of what Kevin needed after a life of hurt. Haven had used his dominance against Kevin, keeping him broken while Haven fell in love with someone else. No one understood what the silent rage had done to him. Now, here was Jericho, being strong and loving. He gave Kevin exactly what he needed.

Jericho shrugged. "You're who I want, and—despite everything—you showed up for me, because you want me too. I'm not calm, sexy. You admitted you love me. This is just me, refusing to be budged. There's a huge difference."

"I'm so sorry." Kevin's voice shook. "I should've been telling you every day that you're the only one for me. I should have..." Kevin grasped for the right words.

"Me too," Jericho said, taking him by surprise. "In my heart, I've known since Vegas that you're special. I'm not the kind of guy who plays around, obviously," he added with a blush. "I don't want to lose you." The words sounded harsh—like they hurt. Kevin got it, because he felt the same.

Kevin swallowed past the hurt that had choked him through the night as he called and called with no answer. "Is it okay if I touch you now?"

Jericho nodded, looking solemn. "I really wish you would."

"Thank god." The breathless words burst from Kevin as he set the roses on the counter and closed the distance between them.

Jericho walked into his arms. Kevin ignored the pains in his chest. He had Jericho. Nothing else mattered. Jericho pressed his lips to Kevin's neck. "Jesus fucking Christ. How often does this watch beep like this?"

Kevin released a soft chuckle. "It's pretty much been nonstop since Haven showed up yesterday."

"Okay. Let me see." He leaned away enough to take Kevin's wrist and stare at the face of the watch. For what felt like forever, Jericho watched the numbers while Kevin stared at Jericho. Damn. There truly wasn't anyone more beautiful. Kevin could spend the rest of his life looking at Jericho.

"I love you."

Jericho's gaze shifted to Kevin's face. "I love you too, angel. We're going to the hospital."

Kevin blinked. "What?"

Jericho held on to Kevin's arm and headed for the door. "Yep. You heard me. Hospital time. I have to make this decision for people all the time. Today, it's for you. Let's go. Your heart isn't returning to a normal rhythm. I'm not willing to lose you, so let's get this fixed."

"That's not what I want to do with my day."

At his petulant tone, Jericho flashed him a smile.

He was always so strong and in control. "What? You don't want to spend the day with me?"

"Of course, I do."

Jericho didn't slow on his way to his truck. "Then you shouldn't care where we spend our time, as long as we're together."

Kevin couldn't argue with Jericho's assessment. Plus, now that he knew Jericho loved him and he could focus on something beyond his fear of losing the man he loved, Kevin realized he didn't feel so hot. Since Jericho walked away from him yesterday, Kevin hadn't been able to think about anything else. Now he recognized his mistake. He had literally been killing himself.

YEARS OF STAYING COOL UNDER PRESSURE CAME to Jericho's rescue in his time of need. He didn't want to panic Kevin, since his heart was already beating way too fast, but his heart was beating way too fast with no sense of rhythm. Jericho didn't have time to drive casually. He had never been more thankful for having worked for the department long enough to have emergency lights on his truck. Since it was a medical emergency, he was well within his rights to use them and he did. Nothing was getting in the way of him taking care of Kevin. This man was his heart. Jericho wouldn't lose him. With his gaze locked on the road, Jericho weaved through traffic and ran through lights while trying to talk himself down. It seemed like he always had to fear losing the people he loved the most.

"Don't worry, baby. I would never leave you."

Jericho tossed Kevin a wink, doing his damnedest to hide the way he was freaking out inside. "I know, gorgeous. Just humor me." The blare of that goddamn watch told a different story.

Without an ounce of shame, Jericho pulled into the ambulance bay and grabbed a gurney. He saw several familiar faces and had no trouble getting Kevin help. In a surprisingly short time, Jericho was through triage and in a private trauma room. No one questioned Jericho staying at Kevin's side. Jericho waffled between thinking he should call Kevin's parents and not wanting to worry them. Oddly, Kevin looked completely relaxed by comparison.

Four hours and countless tests later, a tall, dark-haired man in a white doctor's coat stepped into the room with a laptop tucked beneath his arm. He eyed Kevin as he pulled a rolling stool close to the edge of the bed.

"We have to stop meeting like this, Dr. Tate."

The doctor shook his head at Kevin's too bright tone. "I'd ask how you're doing, Kevin, but I see you've been disobeying my orders to live a calm, stress-free life."

The guilt was real. Jericho knew Kevin had heart problems and still he had walked away from Kevin's argument with Haven. He had refused to answer Kevin's calls and texts, intentionally hurting him. Jericho felt like the worst person. He had come so close to losing his son and he had hurt someone else's. Jericho lost himself in his inner attempts at kicking his own ass. He missed part of the conversation with the doctor. Jericho forced himself to pay attention.

"I'd like to add two more meds to your day. The first one blocks bad signals to the heart and the other is a blood thinner. While the first one should stop your heart from beating out of rhythm, you're still a high risk for stroke. The blood thinner should cut down that risk. I'll send you home with some info on both."

"When can I go home?"

A kind-looking smile stretched the doctor's lips. His eyes crinkled in the corners, proving he smiled a lot. "I don't know if I can trust you to go home. This isn't the first time I've had to fuss at you about looking out for yourself first." His expression turned serious. "You have a deadly heart rhythm, Kevin. This is reality for you. You don't have the option to keep living a high-pressure life. Everyone knows stress kills, but in your case, that's doubly true. If I let you go home, you have to take some time off, and I don't mean working from home. Time off. Feet up. No stress."

"I won't let him do anything," Jericho said, speaking up. This was his fault. He would take care of Kevin.

Dr. Tate's gaze moved Jericho's way. His light brown eyes dropped to Jericho's work clothes. "Austin Fire department, huh? I can't imagine your schedule will let you watch him twenty-four-seven."

"Twenty-five years of service has given me some perks. I can take some time off. He won't be doing anything, even if I have to tie him to the bed."

Kevin's mouth lifted in one corner. He looked like he was fighting back a laugh. Dr. Tate had no idea how easily Jericho could strap him to the headboard. Jericho wasn't joking.

Dr. Tate's gaze moved between them. "Okay. If you promise to make him relax for at least a week and get his meds filled on the way home, I'll get the discharge papers started."

"I plan to make him relax for two weeks. He'll hate me by the end."

Kevin snorted.

Jericho ignored him. He would make this up to Kevin. It hurt his chest that he was the reason Kevin was here. He had listened to Kevin proclaiming his love while ignoring the man's health. Jericho didn't deserve him. He was so fucking mad at himself.

"I'll get the paperwork done."

To Kevin's credit, he managed to hold his tongue until they were alone. "Two weeks? Are you seriously going to take two weeks off work?"

"Yes."

"I'll cover your salary, so you don't miss any pay."

Jericho rolled his eyes. "I have vacation time."

Kevin was getting agitated. His heart rate was going up again. "You don't need to waste your vacation time on me."

"Baby," Jericho said, flashing a sweet smile. "I would quit tomorrow and live in a cardboard box to take care of you. Being with you is never a waste. I love you."

"I love you too," Kevin said, sounding solemn. His heart rate dropped again.

Jericho took his hand. "You have to let me do this." His throat swelled. "I need to take care of you." He had to make up for nearly killing his heart. Kevin nodded, sealing his fate. Jericho would be so far up Kevin's ass for the next two weeks, Kevin would beg for peace. He really loved this man. It was time they both worked harder at showing it.

ELEVEN

TO JERICHO'S SURPRISE, Kevin was the perfect patient. If he was the least bit tired of hanging out in bed, or sick of seeing Jericho's face, he never let on. Jericho was the one struggling, but it had nothing to do with being sick of Kevin. In fact, he never wanted to go back to work. It was heaven staying kicked back with Kevin all day, watching movies or just talking nonstop. Every day, Kevin looked brighter. He smiled more. His shoulders relaxed. The hard edge he had always had to his jaw seemed to soften. Jericho had never felt closer to anyone. Sometimes, he wanted to crawl under Kevin's skin to get even closer, which was why he was ready to scream after two weeks in bed. Kevin was supposed to be relaxing. Even though—

technically—the doctor had only ordered one week of rest, Jericho was scared as hell to get Kevin's heart rate up again. It was hell being in the bed all hours of the day and night without making love. Kevin didn't make things any easier.

After a quick shower, Kevin climbed back in bed. The glasses he wore caught and held Jericho's attention.

"Goddamn."

Kevin froze, looking adorably confused at Jericho's lust-filled curse. "I haven't even touched you yet. Why do you sound so breathless?"

Jericho slid closer. He heart needed him to be closer. "It's the glasses. I don't know what is, but they just do it for me. The first time I saw you in them, I was a goner. I can't explain it, but I really can't wait to get inside you. Leave the glasses on." He shook his head, coming back to himself. "Wait. We can't do that. You're supposed to be relaxing. Quick. Take them off."

A sexy rumble of laughter fell from Kevin's lips. "Who would've thought me being half blind is what would make me irresistible. And here I've been slaving away to get rich."

Jericho hummed in delight as Kevin crawled

closer. "You can keep your money, baby. I'm here for the package."

Kevin kept coming until he straddled Jericho's body. Without thought, Jericho's hands went straight to cupping his ass so he could grind Kevin's body against his erection. No shame. Kevin leaned in and stole a quick kiss. "Dr. Tate said a week," Kevin said between kisses. "It's been two. I've been a good boy."

A growl vibrated in Jericho's throat. He rolled and tucked Kevin beneath him while tugging at his clothes. "Yes, you have. You've definitely earned a treat." Jericho fully intended to make him scream.

"I think you should let me have whatever I want."

Jericho froze. His gaze locked on to Kevin at his strange tone. Damn. He really did look sexy beneath Jericho. It was distracting. "Why do I get the feeling this is leading somewhere different than I'm going?"

Kevin's expression shifted. He looked uncomfortable. "Never mind."

Nope. That wasn't happening. Jericho sat back on his heels. "Talk to me, sexy."

"It's stupid. Carry on."

For a full minute, Jericho stared down at Kevin while Kevin squirmed. His heart squeezed at Kevin's discomfort. "Please don't do that. I want us to talk about things, even if it's something we think the other one won't like. Maybe especially then."

Kevin ran his hands up Jericho's thighs. His sexy bare chest kept distracting Jericho. He wanted to run his hands through all that chest hair. It called his name.

"It's just that I don't want to go back to not holding you at night." Kevin sounded sad.

Damn. Jericho hadn't really thought about going home. He had slept better than he had in years while sleeping in Kevin's arms every night for the past two weeks. Jericho sucked in a hiss. "Yeah. That's a depressing thought. I remember my bed being really empty without you."

A sweet smile touched Kevin's lips. "Move in with me." Before Jericho could respond, Kevin fell into a babbling that didn't fit with him. Jericho was normally the one who panicked. "I'm not saying you have to give up everything—like if you want to keep your house and rent it out or something, that's cool. I understand you might not feel like you can depend on me forever. You probably don't have a lot of faith in a guy who has divorce papers with barely dried ink. It's just that I love you and I truly believe we're in this for the long haul." Kevin took an audible breath, as if trying to stop. "I just want to go to bed with you for the rest of my life. You are the best part of me," Kevin added, squeezing Jericho's thighs.

The oddest thought hit Jericho and he couldn't stop it from falling from his lips. "You should completely terrify me. I mean, you one hundred percent torpedoed into my life and stole me. But, for whatever reason, I'm not frightened at all."

"I'm not finished yet." Kevin's claim came out sounding quiet and serious—like a warning. "From the first night we talked all night, it's been my plan to completely own every inch of you. I want your life tied so tightly to mine that you can't get away. Hell, I need your life to be a permanent piece of me, because being without you would kill me. You're right. You should be terrified. I'll do anything to keep you."

It was insane to Jericho that he had made it to forty-five without feeling an ounce of what he felt for Kevin for anyone else. His love for Loyal was different, but it was also the only emotion comparable to what he felt for Kevin. Just as he knew his son's love was unbreakable, Jericho knew Kevin would never disappoint him. "I swear I'll make your life everything you never dreamed it could be."

"You already have," Kevin said, luring Jericho down for a kiss.

Jericho's entire body went on the alert, humming with anticipation. As their lips met and their tongues brushed, Jericho embraced his fate. He had always possessed a loyal soul. He attached to one person and dug his heels in until there was nothing left to cling to, and Kevin was no different. He had spent his entire life waiting for something he couldn't name. Jericho hadn't known what he was missing. He only knew it was something. Turned out, it was someone. Kevin completed Jericho. Everything looked brighter now than it had before him. This was his happily ever after. As Kevin's hand slipped inside Jericho's pajama pants, Jericho amended his thoughts. Forever with Kevin would always come with a happy ending.

BEING HIRED TO DEMO FOR DEX WISE, a billionaire known for creating reality TV shows that had rabid followings, was a bit intimidating. While his friend Orion had predicted Haven's BDSM demos would become a growing trend and make Haven rich, Haven didn't believe anyone at Cubs for Rent had been prepared for how in demand Haven would be. Since he did upwards of five demos a night on the weekends, he had gotten pretty good at transporting his gear from one job to the next. He had just spent an hour at Dex Wise's house, rubbing elbows with the stars. That was one place Haven never expected to be. Dex Wise was a billionaire TV genius. He was the man behind countless explosive reality shows. Haven had no idea why the guy had hired him. Haven had spent his hour-long demonstration talking to a crowd of guests who pretended he wasn't there as they milled around chatting. It was uncomfortable but familiar. Haven was getting used to being invisible. He froze with one hand on the lid of his trunk and the other on his work bag. His mind drifted.

I wish you were dead. Those words were never far from Haven's thoughts. Every time his mind went there, he could see his ex Kevin's face. He could picture Kevin's hatred and feel the punch to his chest as if it just happened. Haven couldn't fall over dead and give Kevin his wish, but he could and would kill his heart. He owed Kevin that much. Haven deserved to be alone for the rest of his life with his guilt. The more he sequestered himself from others, the less people noticed his presence. It was fucking odd. He wished he didn't still miss Kevin so much.

"You dropped this on the way out the door."

As the sultry words washed over Haven, he

shook himself from the black hole trying to suck him under. He focused on the polished blond angel. The boy, who couldn't be more than twenty, held out one of Haven's crops. Haven pasted on a fake smile and reached for it.

"Thank you. I didn't even notice."

Light green eyes sparkled with life, good humor, and a certain level of naughtiness. "It's no problem. I was headed this way anyhow. As a policy, I always leave Dex's parties before the real perverts turn up, and I have another job to get to." Before Haven could inquire, the boy spoke over him. "You work for Cubs for Rent, right? Me too. I'm Wren."

Haven held out his hand for Wren to shake. "Charmed. I'm Haven."

Wren's eyebrow rose. Just the one. There was so much cockiness in the gesture that Haven fought a laugh. This one was trouble. "Haven? I thought your name was Mister."

"I go by both," Haven admitted. "I'm an author. Mister Haven is my pen name." He didn't bother explaining Mister was something subs called him. That was in his past.

"Where are you off to now?" Wren asked, moving past the name issue.

Haven checked his watch. "I believe my next job is in Rosedale. What about you?"

A spark of challenge entered Wren's eyes. "I'm a dancer at the Woodshed. I'd invite you to come see me, but I'm afraid you might spank me for being bad." He winked.

Despite Wren's over-the-top flirtatious personality, Haven couldn't stop smiling. "You don't have to worry. I don't spank people anymore."

"Shame."

A chuckle escaped Haven. "I don't hang out at places called the Woodshed either."

A mock gasp escaped Wren. "Scandal. Well, I guess I'll just go then before I taint you with my hussiness."

"Is that a word?"

"It is now," Wren said, taking a step backward.

Despite his best efforts, Haven couldn't stop his gaze from skimming Wren's body. He was breathtaking and trouble. Haven could smell that last bit from a mile away.

Wren's smile hitched up a notch. "I saw that."

"What?" Haven tried looking as innocent as possible.

"Mhmm," Wren hummed, not bothering to say what they both knew. Haven had been checking him out. He turned away but took one last parting shot over his shoulder. "No staring at my ass. You're above such things."

Haven bit his bottom lip to keep from laughing. His smile refused to be controlled. He shook his head as he slipped behind the wheel of his car. With no input from his brain, Haven's gaze slid Wren's way again. Wow. His ass was perfect.

Keep an eye out for the next Cubs for Rent, *Until Mister*.

PLEASE CONSIDER LEAVING A REVIEW AT THE retailer where this book was purchased. Reviews really help with a book's visibility, which ensures I can continue writing. Thank you, Charity.

ABOUT THE AUTHOR

Charity Parkerson is an award winning and multi-published author with several companies. Born with no filter from her brain to her mouth, she decided to take this odd quirk and insert it in her characters.

*Eight-time Readers' Favorite Award Winner

   *2015 Passionate Plume Award Finalist

   *2013 Reviewers' Choice Award Winner

   *2012 ARRA Finalist for Favorite Paranormal Romance

   *Five-time winner of The Mistress of the Darkpath

Connect with her online:

--Join my street team: facebook.com/TeamCharityParkerson

   --Website: charityparkerson.com

   --Facebook: facebook.com/authorCharityParkerson

facebook.com/TheMenofSin

--Twitter: twitter.com/CharityParkerso

www.ingramcontent.com/pod-product-compliance
Lightning Source LLC
Chambersburg PA
CBHW061239170626
46809CB00007B/2740